* * * * * * *

"We are having a problem with buffalo hunters. They are killing off the buffalo, and I can tell you it's going to be a real big problem if we don't do something about it soon."

"I didn't think killing buffalo was against the law."

"It's not, and that's the problem.

"I don't understand," Bender said.

"The problem is they are killing the buffalo just for their skins, and leaving the carcasses to rot in the sun. By the time the Indians get to the carcasses, they are too spoiled to eat."

"So, what you're saying is, the buffalo hunters are taking food right out of the Indians' mouths, so to speak," Bender said.

"That's about the best way I have heard it said. If the buffalo hunters continue to kill the buffalo at the rate they are now, there will not be any buffalo left on the plains in less than five years."

* * * * * * *

Other titles by J.E. Terrall

Western Short Stories
  The Old West*
  The Frontier*
  Untamed Land*
  Tales from the Territory*
  Frontier Justice*

Western Novels
  Conflict in Elkhorn Valley*
  Lazy A Ranch
    (A Modern Western)
  The Story of Joshua Higgins*
  The Valley Ranch War*
  Jake Murdock, Bounty Hunter*

Romance Novels
  Balboa Rendezvous
  Sing for Me*
  Return to Me*
  Forever Yours*

Mystery/Suspense/Thriller
  I Can See Clearly*
  The Return Home*
  The Inheritance

Bill Sparks Mysteries
  Murder in the Backcountry*   Murder and the Gold Coins*

Nick McCord Mysteries
  Vol – 1 Murder at Gill's Point
  Vol – 2 Death of a Flower
  Vol – 3 A Dead Man's Treasure
  Vol – 4 Blackjack, A Game to Die For
  Vol – 5 Death on the Lakes
  Vol – 6 Secrets Can Get You Killed
  Vol – 7 Murder on the Racetrack

Peter Blackstone Mysteries
  Murder in the Foothills
  Murder on the Crystal Blue
  Murder of My Love
  Murder in the Dark of Night

Frank Tidsdale Mysteries
  Death by Design
  Death by Assassination

Non-fiction:
Two Brothers Go To War/Letters from WWI

*Also available in Large Print Editions

VANISHING WILDERNESS

A collection of Western short stories

by
J.E. Terrall

All Rights Reserved
Copyright © 2022 by J.E. Terrall

ISBN: 978-0-9997823-9-2

No part of this book may be reproduced or transmitted in any form or by any means, electronic or mechanical, including photocopying, recording or by any information storage or retrieval system, in whole or in part, without the expressed written consent of the author.

This is a work of fiction. Names, characters, and incidents are either a product of the author's imagination or are used fictitiously, and any resemblance to actual persons, living or dead, is purely coincidental.

Printed in the United States of America
First Printing / 2022 – www.kdp.com

Cover: Front and back covers by author, J.E. Terrall

Book Layout /
Formatting: J.E. Terrall
              Custer, South Dakota

VANISHING WILDERNESS

A collection of Western short stories

To
Steve Wood,
one of my best fans, and
a good promoter and friend.

VANISHING WILDERNESS

Where the Buffalo Once Roamed........9

The Ghost Town of Dustyville 25

Out of the Wilderness................ 37

Marshal Sam Phillips 53

In a Strange Land 65

The Capture of Ben Sulley 79

Zackery Johnson, Government Agent . . 91

Life After the War.................. 103

Lone Tree Station....................121

Wells Fargo Robbery 137

WHERE THE BUFFALO ONCE ROAMED

While in Omaha, Bender Wilson had received a letter from a government representative for the Indian Agency located in Lincoln, Nebraska. The letter was an offer of a job, but didn't say much about the job. It simply said that there was a job waiting for him. Since Bender didn't have anything else to do at the moment, and he was a little short of funds, he decided to find out what kind of a job it might be. The letter was signed by George Morris. The fact that Bender knew George Morris might have had something to do with Bender deciding to go to Lincoln to find out what it was George wanted him to do.

Bender knew that his old friend, George Morris, was in charge of Indian affairs at the Indian Agency in Lincoln. He figured the job might have something to do with the Indians. Bender had worked with a few Indian chiefs during his time as a scout for the Army. He was sure that George knew he had a good relationship with most of the chiefs in the area. Bender decided he would spend the night in Omaha, then head for Lincoln in the morning.

When morning came, Bender packed up his meager possessions. He walked down to the Blacksmith's shop and stable. After paying for the keep of his horse, Bender put his saddlebags, bedroll and rifle on the saddle. He put his foot in the stirrup, swung into the saddle then set out for Lincoln, Nebraska.

Bender figured it would take him almost two weeks to get to Lincoln. While traveling across the Nebraska Territory, he took in his surroundings. The first couple of days, he saw several small farms, but they became fewer and farther between as he moved further west. The prairie grasses seemed to be in good shape. He didn't see a lot of buffalo, but didn't really expect to see very many in eastern Nebraska. However, he did see a good number of antelope.

It didn't take Bender very long, a little over a week, to get to Lincoln. He rode up and tied his horse in front of the Indian Agency's office. He looked around a little, then went into the office. George Morris looked up from his desk just as Bender walked in the door.

"I didn't expect to see you so soon," George said as he stood up and reached out his hand. "I guess I expected you to drop me a line to ask me what kind of job I was offering you."

"I would have, but I was in Omaha when your letter arrived," Bender said as they shook hands. "I found your letter rather interesting even if you didn't tell me what kind of a job you had for me. You want to tell me about the job?"

"You haven't changed a bit. You always have been one to look at the unknown with interest. You also get right to the point. Have a seat and I'll tell you what I have in mind."

They sat down before George said anything more. He looked at Bender for a moment before he spoke.

"Are you aware of what is going on with the buffalo hunters?"

"Not really. I haven't given them much thought at all. I've had very little contact with any of them. Why don't you fill me in?"

"We are having a problem with buffalo hunters. They are killing off the buffalo, and I can tell you it's going to be a real big problem if we don't do something about it soon."

"I didn't think killing buffalo was against the law."

"It's not, and that's the problem."

"I don't understand," Bender said.

"The problem is they are killing the buffalo just for their hides, and leaving the carcasses to rot. By the time the Indians get to the carcasses they are too spoiled to provide food food for them."

"So, what you're saying is, the buffalo hunters are taking food right out of the Indians' mouths, so to speak," Bender said.

"That's about the best way I have heard it said. But that is just what they are doing. If the buffalo hunters continue to kill the buffalo at the rate they are now, there will not be any buffalo left on the plains in less than five years. The buffalo is the Indians way of life. You know as well as I do that when you try to take away people's way of life, you can expect them to fight back, which means a lot of people will be getting killed, both Indians and white men if something isn't done. The military does not have the manpower to stop it," George added.

"I see your problem and understand it, but just what do you think I can do about it?"

"I don't know if you can do anything, but I would like you to try."

"You have some ideas that might help me figure a way to help solve this problem?"

"First of all, I would like you to talk to the buffalo hunters and see if there is some way to, at the very least, get them to slow down the killing of buffalo."

"What makes you think I can do anything to stop them when they are not breaking the law? As I see it, they are no different from the Indians. You are trying to take away their way of life, too."

"I know. That's part of what makes this so hard. You have spent a good number of years as a scout for the Army in the Dakota, Nebraska, and Kansas Territories. You probably know more about what goes on out on the plains than anyone else. You have dealt with Indians and white men who live out there. Maybe you can convince some of the buffalo hunters that it is in their own best interest, as well as for the good of the Indians, to stop killing every buffalo they see."

"You've got to be kidding. Do you have any idea what you're asking?"

"I think I do. I'm sure that it won't be easy."

"That's for sure. Buffalo hunters are some of the toughest men you will ever meet. You think they are going to give up their way of life on my say so?"

"No. But I'm not kidding. I know what I'm asking is not going to be easy," George said.

"Just how do you expect me to get them together to work things out?"

"I don't know, but I need time."

"Time to do what?"

"I need time to convince the congress in Washington to create laws preventing the continual slaughter of buffalo. At least until such a law can be put on the books."

"How have things been going at getting Washington to even listen to you?" Bender asked.

"I have to admit, it is not going well. In fact, the last time I talked to them, they basically laughed at me, but most of the time they just don't even listen.

"A good deal of them don't care what happens to the Indians. The problem is those in Washington don't have any interest in what goes on out west of the Mississippi River, unless it effects their chances of getting elected."

"I figure I'll have about that same luck with the buffalo hunters as you have had with those in Washington. The difference being, I doubt the buffalo hunters will just laugh or ignore me. Most likely, their answer will probably be a lot harsher and probably a lot more violent than just not listening.

"I'll be face to face with some very hard men, and asking them to give up their way of making a living. I'll be lucky if they just tar and feather me. I will probably get the same reaction from them you would get from the Indians."

"I know, but we have to try. I'll give you as much support as I can. If we don't do something soon, we could very well have an Indian uprising on our hands," George said.

Bender sat there just looking at George. He was trying to come up with something that just might work. Suddenly, an idea came to him.

"George, do you think the Indians could raise buffalo if they had a small herd to start out with?"

Bender could see that George was thinking about what he was suggesting. It had never been suggested before. Bender also doubted that it would work, but the idea was no worse than what George was suggesting.

"How would it work?" George asked.

"We would gather up a small herd of buffalo and put them on the reservation where the buffalo hunters could not hunt them. The Indians would raise the buffalo much the same way cattlemen raise cattle. They would have to keep them in numbers high enough to help feed the people of the tribe. Only killing off what they needed, and keep the herd so it could continue to provide them with meat. Ranchers do it with cattle, even raising enough to sell off some at the end of the year," Bender explained.

"It sounds like a good idea, but it would mean a change in the Indians' way of life," George said.

"I know, but isn't their way of life already changing? They are being put on reservations, isn't that changing their way of life?"

"I see your point."

"Do you think the Indians would go along with it?"

"I don't know. They are having enough problems not being able to roam the prairie as they had been for hundreds of years. They might go along with it if I can convince them they would have buffalo for a very long time. I will certainly talk to the chiefs about it," George said.

"Good. I'll go out and see if I can find some buffalo hunters and talk to them. I'll try to convince them that it is good for them, too. If they keep hunting the buffalo the way they are, they won't have buffalo to hunt for very long. Maybe I can convince them that their way of life is rapidly going to change with the loss of the buffalo anyway. I doubt they will listen to me, but they might." Bender said. "I'm willing to give it a try."

"Thanks. I was hoping you would at least try."

"I'll try, but I can't say it will do any good," Bender said.

"That is all I'm asking. It is more than what I have going for me now."

Bender stood up, shook hands with George, then turned and left the office. He looked up and down the street, before he swung up in the saddle and headed for the Blacksmith's shop and stable. After leaving his horse with the blacksmith to take care of, he went to the hotel to get a good meal and some much-needed rest before he would start out in the morning.

When morning came, Bender went to a café and had a good meal. He then went to the blacksmith's shop and paid for the care of his horse. As soon as he had what he needed, he left Lincoln. He headed west out onto the prairie.

Days past as he continued on west looking for signs of large herds of buffalo. He also looked for signs of a wagon or two that were not on the usual trails taken by most of the wagon trains. Those would probably be the wagons of buffalo hunters.

Bender had been gone from Lincoln for about eight days when he came to a hill that was just a little higher than most of the surrounding prairie. He rode up on top of the hill. He stopped and sat in the saddle as he looked around. Off in the distance he thought he could see something that looked like carcasses of buffalo. He reached back to his saddlebags and took his field glasses out of his saddlebags. Bender put his field glasses up to his eyes and scanned the area.

What he saw simply amazed him. He saw at least a hundred buffalo that had been skinned, and their remains left to rot in the sun. He continued to scan the area in an effort to see if there was anyone around. He saw no one.

Bender put his field glasses back in his saddlebags and rode down off the hill. He rode toward where the buffalo carcasses had been left. When he got close, his horse didn't like the smell of the rotting buffalo. He rode around so the breeze was coming toward the buffalo and away from his horse. Bender got off his horse and tied it to a nearby scrub oak.

As soon as his horse was secure, he began walking among the buffalo. It bothered him that nothing had been taken from the buffalo but their hides, and that the meat of the buffalo was simply left to rot. It was easy for him to see why the Indians would be angry at whoever caused such a waste.

Bender mounted up and began following the tracks left by the buffalo hunter's wagon. It didn't take Bender long to find the buffalo hunters. They had only gone about five miles from the buffalo he had seen. It was getting on toward noon when he saw them sitting around a campfire. He decided to ride up and talk to them.

As he got close, Bender could see that they were watching him. Two of the men went around behind the wagon. Bender was sure they were not going to be friendly. When he was only about twenty-five yards from them, they called out.

"That's close enough."

"My name's Bender Wilson. I would like to talk to you."

"What about?"

"About buffalo hunting."

"You one of them do-gooders who want me to stop hunting buffalo so the Indians can have them?"

"No, but I would like to talk to you about your future as a buffalo hunter."

"You ain't got anything to say to me that ain't been said already. The last guy that tried to stop me from huntin' buffalo, didn't fare so well. I suggest you move on before we have to bury you right here."

"I'm not here to get into a fight with you. I'll just say, that at the rate you and your fellow buffalo hunters are killing off the buffalo, you will be out of a job before long."

Bender turned his horse around and rode off. It was clear that there was no talking to this buffalo hunter. He would have to see the end result for himself, by then it would be too late.

It was also clear that their wagon was empty. Bender was sure that they had not been the ones who killed and skinned the buffalo he had seen. It crossed his mind that the buffalo hunters he just talked to were a bit angry because they had not gotten to the buffalo first.

Bender rode about a mile, then turned north. He didn't see any buffalo or buffalo hunters for several miles.

After several days of not seeing anyone, Bender came upon a deserted campsite. He got off his horse and began looking for tracks. He discovered wagon tracks, and the hoof prints of at least six animals. Once he found the tracks of the wagon, he decided that he would follow them in the hope of finding where they were camping.

It was getting on toward sunset when he found where they had camped. He was able to determine that there were five men, two wagons, two horses and at least four mules. The mules were used to pull the two wagons, and the wagons were probably full of hides.

He also discovered that the wagon tracks looked like they had been heading generally in a northwest direction. The only trading post northwest of there where they could possibly sell the hides was near Fort McPherson along the Platt River.

Bender returned to his horse and began following the tracks left by the wagons and the two riders. He hoped to catch up with the buffalo hunters before they reached the trading post. He was sure he had a good chance of catching up with them since their tracks were fresh, and they were not moving very fast.

By the end of the second day of following the buffalo hunters, he spotted them near a small grove of cottonwood trees along a creek. It looked like they were going to stop for the night.

Bender wasn't sure how he was going to approach them. He wasn't even sure what he was going to say to them. He had not had any luck trying to talk to the last buffalo hunters he came across. They had simply threatened to shoot him if he didn't leave.

After giving it some thought, he decided that he would ride up to their camp. Bender hoped to get them into a discussion on the future of the buffalo, and the future of the buffalo hunter. He doubted it would be as easy as it sounded, but maybe a more direct approach would work.

Bender nudged his horse on toward the buffalo hunters' camp. When he was close enough to be heard, he called out to them.

"Howdy. Can I come into your camp?"

He noticed that two of the men stood up and put their hands on their guns, though they didn't draw them. A third just sat there and looked toward him. Another looked like he might be the cook. He just stood next to the fire and looked toward Bender.

Bender knew that there were five men. He had four of them in front of him. He wondered where the fifth man was. It wasn't but a minute or so before he found out.

"I don't know who you are, but I got you covered," came a voice off to the side and in the dark where he could not be seem.

"I'm not here to cause you any trouble. I just thought I might get a cup of coffee and visit awhile," Bender said. "I haven't seen anyone for several days. But if you don't want me here, I'll just turn my horse around and go on my way."

"Where you headed?" the man sitting down asked.

"I'm an Army scout. I'm headed for Fort McPherson."

"What was ya scoutin'?"

"I was traveling around looking for Indians mostly."

"Why ya doin' that?"

"It seems we got a bunch of Indians that want to cause some problems. Seems they are rather upset."

"What kind of problems? And what are they upset about?"

Bender noticed that the man sitting down was doing all the talking. It was clear that he was the boss of this outfit. It was also clear that he was interested in what the Indians might be doing. That was understandable. He probably had an idea, at least, of what the Indians would do if they caught them with just the hides of buffalo.

"They're upset about buffalo hunters killing the buffalo and taking just their hides. The buffalo are their main source of meat and warm clothes as well as a lot of other uses."

"That may be, but it ain't agin' the law ta hunt buffalo for their hides."

"No, it is not. Would you mind if I get down out of this saddle and sit awhile? I've been in the saddle all day long."

The man sitting down on the ground looked at the others. No one made a move to object.

"Get down and sit a spell."

"My name is Bender Wilson. If you don't mind my asking, what's your name?"

"I've heard of you. I'm Clint Connor, but most people just call me, Big Clint. I'm head of this mangey bunch."

"Jesse, get a cup of coffee for our friend."

Bender watched a tall young man take his hand off his gun then step over near the fire. The man tending to the fire, poured a cup of coffee and gave it to Jesse. Jesse then handed the cup to Bender.

"Thanks." Bender said as he took the cup.

Once Jesse turned away, Bender turned to look at Clint."

"I hope you don't mind, but I've got a question for you, Clint."

"Sure thing. What's your question?"

"I'd like to know how long it took you to get all the hides you have in your wagons?"

"What you want ta know that for?"

"I'm just interested. You see, I ran across a small herd of buffalo the other day that had been killed and skinned a while back. It looked to be about a hundred of them."

"That was the herd that all the hides we got come from."

"I kinda figured that. How long were you out here looking before you came upon the buffalo?"

"Well, let me see, it's been about eight or nine weeks 'fore we come across that herd."

"Did you see any other herds?"

"No, as a matter of fact we didn't. Say, what are you gettin' at? You some sort of lawman?"

"No. I travel the plains a lot, mostly for the Army. The one thing I've been noticing is that there are a lot fewer buffalo out here on the plains than in the past years. It seems to me that at the rate they are being hunted, it won't take much longer and there won't be enough buffalo to make it worth hunting them."

Big Clint just looked at Bender while he rubbed his chin. He was thinking about what Bender had said. He was beginning to think back at his other buffalo hunting trips, too.

"Now that I think about it, it has taken us a lot longer ta find that herd of buffalo."

"Think about this. If it keeps going like it has been, buffalo hunting will become so difficult that it won't be worth doing. It will soon cost more than it is worth. You won't even be able to make enough money to pay your crew, let along make a profit."

Clint just looked at Bender for a minute. As much as he didn't like it, Bender seemed to be making a lot of sense. For the past couple of years, it had been harder to make it worth the time and effort. Each year was harder than the year before.

"Ya know, when I take the time ta think about it, you might just have somethin' there. The problem is how do I make a livin' if I can't hunt buffalo? Ya got an answer for that?"

Clint just looked at Bender to see if he had an answer to that question.

"No, no I don't. But, you know. When I think about it, I just might have a possible answer, maybe more of a suggestion. That is if you want to hear it. However, what comes to mind at the moment might not be to your liking. You may want to think about it for awhile."

"Okay. Give it a shot. I'm willin' ta listen. If I think it's worth it, I might even think about it," Clint said with a grin.

"Okay, that sounds fair. First of all, how much do you think the hides you have are worth in cash?"

"Well, I guess their worth some wheres around, maybe a thousand dollars, maybe a slight bit more at taday's prices. What ya gettin' at?"

"Suppose you were to take that money and use part of it to buy a parcel of land. Actually, in the right place, you could get some land for free from the government."

"The government is given away land? I find that hard ta believe."

"It's true. They passed a law called The Homestead Act awhile back. All you have to do is go to one of the government land offices and find out where they have free land. There is a land office in Omaha, and I think there is one in Lincoln. Then you make a claim on a parcel of land. But there is a hitch."

"Okay, what kind of a hitch?" he asked suspiciously.

"You have to do five hundred dollars worth of improvements on the land. Building a house to live in would cover that, and you have to live on the land for five years. Once you have done those two things, the land is yours free and clear," Bender explained.

"You funnin' me?" Clint asked.

Clint suddenly got serious. He didn't like someone making fun of him.

"No. No, I'm not. After five years, it is your land free and clear."

"How much land could we get?"

"One hundred and sixty acres."

Bender could see that Clint was starting to think about it.

"Could each of my boys get one hundred and sixty acres," he asked.

"I don't know, but if they are adults, they might. If they are married, certainly they could, but they would have to file for their plot of land separately from yours."

"Jesse, Joey, you been listenin' ta what Bender been sayin'?"

Each of the boys nodded that they had heard what was said.

"What do you boys think?" Bender asked.

"I think it is something we should look inta, Pa," Joey said. "I'm getting tired of all the time we spend out here and not seein' anythin'."

"I sure would like ta have a place of our own." Jesse said. "Buffalo hunting is getting harder. A place where we could raise cattle or farm would be all right with me."

"What does it cost us ta file for this land?" Clint asked.

"I don't think there is a fee, but you will have to sign an agreement that says if you don't do five hundred dollars in improvements in five years, you lose the land. But you can farm it or raise cattle on it. Whatever you decide to do with the land, and make the required improvements, the land will be yours at the end of five years. And that is free and clear land."

"Would each of us that files for a claim have ta do five hundred dollars in improvement on our claim?" Jesse asked.

"Yes, but it doesn't take a lot to make five hundred dollars in improvements. Build a house, or a barn would do it."

Bender could see that Clint was thinking real hard about the idea. Then his face sort of lit up.

"If we each file for a parcel of land, and it's free land, we would still have the money from the hides? Right?"

"Right."

Clint looked at his boys. It was easy to see that he was thinking about what Bender had said. He had heard about Bender. What he had heard made him think that Bender was telling them the truth.

"Boys, I won't speak for you, but I think this is my last buffalo hunt. What do ya say?"

"Pa," Jesse said. "If we all go tagether maybe we could get parcels of land that are close tagether. I'm with you."

"I'm more than willin' to give up buffalo hunting even if we can't get parcels of land that would be tagether," Joey said. "It would be nice, but maybe we can get them at least close enough so we could work together and help each other."

"I guess this is our last buffalo hunt, Bender. The rest of ya will get paid and then ya can do whatever you want."

"I think I might do something else, too," one of the hired hands said. "Maybe get myself a piece of land and maybe one of them mail order brides I hear talk about."

"What about you, cooky?" Clint asked.

"I might join one of these wagon trains passin' through, and take a look at what's out west." he said with a grin. "Might even find me a wife."

Bender spent the night with Clint and his crew. In the morning, he bid Clint and his men 'goodbye' and went on looking for other buffalo hunters.

Bender was no fool. He knew he would not get the same results with other buffalo hunters he got with Clint and his crew, but at least he had gotten one group of hunters to stop hunting the buffalo. Maybe he could get others to give up buffalo hunting. Only time would tell.

Bender continued to look for buffalo hunters and talk to them. He got a couple of them to at least think about their future as buffalo hunters, but many of them refused to listen about the future of buffalo hunting as a means of making a living.

Historical note: The buffalo, or American Bison, were hunted almost to extinction. One buffalo hunter, who had hunted buffalo to feed the crews building the Transcontinental railroad across the country, built a ranch near North Platte, Nebraska, where he raised buffalo. That buffalo hunter was Willian Cody, aka Buffalo Bill. His ranch is now Buffalo Bill Ranch State Historic Park.

THE GHOST TOWN OF DUSTYVILLE

It was mid-September of 1889 when the sun was about to set on three travelers. The three men were weary and covered with the dust and dirt of many miles of hard riding. The tired men slowly rode across the southwestern desert in the Arizona Territory toward what appeared to be a small town.

Their horses were also covered with the dust and dirt of many miles of hard traveling, and were feeling it. The horses were just plain wore-out. Their heads were down and their pace was slow. The weather had turned cold for mid-September, but the weather was often cold at night in the Arizona desert even when it had been hot during the day.

The sun had already set when the travelers finally arrived at the edge of a small town. A full moon was just starting to creep up over the horizon causing long, weird looking shadows that spread out over the barren land.

At the edge of the small desert town was a sign that hung sideways on a post by a single rusty nail. One of the men rode up to the sign, reached down and turned it so he could read it. The paint on the sign was so faded it was difficult to read. The rider stepped out of the saddle to get a better look at the sign.

The rider walked up to the sign while the other two men sat on their horses and watched him. He turned the sign so he could read it.

"This here town is, or I should say, was called 'Dustyville'. From the look of thin's, it was a good name for this place," he said.

"Get back on your horse," the older man said. "We'll check it out. It might be a good place to hunker down so these horses can rest a bit."

The man got back on his horse and the three men rode on into the ghost town of Dustyville. As they rode along the street, they saw the wind blowing tumble weeds back and forth across the street, and in between the buildings. Some of the tumble weeds rolled across the boardwalks while some piled up in front of the doors of the deserted buildings.

The buildings in the abandoned town showed the wear of a good many years of wind and sand blowing against them, as well as the dust storms that had battered the buildings of the town. The shadows of the abandoned buildings gave an eerie, almost spooky look to the town.

The front of one of the buildings had a sign that read "Bank of Dustyville". The front door on the bank hung open and loosely on a single hinge. Most of the glass in the front window was broken out.

The door on the general store was swinging back and forth in the wind, slamming each time it swung closed making a lot of noise. It was almost as if it was beckoning someone to come into the building to buy something.

The eerie sounds of the wind whistling through the old buildings made it sound like the buildings were crying out in pain, or they were calling out to the ghosts of the night to come and visit them.

The three men rode slowly along the street. Dust swirled around the hoofs of their horses as they plodded along. The horses were as tired at the men who rode them.

The three men looked around as they slowly moved along the only street in the town. As the riders approached the bank, they pulled up in front of the building. One of the men got off his horse and stepped up on the boardwalk. As he walked up to the window, he kicked a few tumble weeds out of the way. He got to the window of the bank and looked inside.

Although it was dark, in the moonlight he could see that the bank was empty. Even the safe was wide open. There were tumble weeds piled up in front of the teller's cage as if waiting for the teller to wait on them.

There was noise from one of the night critters as it scurrying across the floor in an effort to find a place to hide from the strangers. The critter startled the man causing him to jump back. He turned around and looked at his partners still sitting on their mounts. They were grinning at him.

"That there little critter startled me. It seems he thinks it's his bank."

"Ya see anythin' of interest in there?" the older man asked.

"I don't see anythin' we could use. I guess we can't rob this bank. It don't look like this bank has any money in it," Donny said with a chuckle.

"Get back on your horse. I think we'll spend the night here," the older man said.

"Pa, you think that's a good idea?" Billy asked as he looked around.

Billy's voice sounded like he might be a little scared of this strange town and of the ghosts might be living there. The look on his face as he looked around gave a hint of how nervous he was about even being in this ghost town.

"What's a matter Billy, you scared there might be ghosts in this here ghost town," Donny said laughingly."

"You makin' fun of me, Donny?" Billy said as he slid his hand down over his gun.

"Nah. I was just funnin' ya, brother."

"You boys knock it off. We're goin' ta spend a couple of days here. The horses are plum near wore out. If'n we don't let um rest up a bit before we head in ta Mexico, we might not make it ta Mexico."

"You think we got a good enough lead on that marshal fella?" Billy asked. "He seemed pretty well set on followin' us. Last we seen of him, he ain't showed no signs of slowin' down.

"I'd be willin' ta bet he's turned back by now. He didn't have no supplies so's he could follow us across this desert. If'n he tried, he weren't goin' to make it this far, anyways."

"Where we goin' ta bed down, Pa?"

"It looks ta me that we have the whole town to find a place to bed down. Billy, you got your pick of any of the buildin's you want. You pick out one and it's all yours," Donny said.

Billy didn't say anything. Looking around, he couldn't see any place where he was sure he could get any real rest. This place was spooky to him. It made him nervous. He didn't like it one bit.

"Look down there. It looks like it might be a barn. If'n it is, we can put the horses up there outa of this wind and dust," Billy said.

"That's a good idea, Billy. There might even be a little hay left for um," Pa said. "Let's head on down there."

The three rode on down the street to the barn. When they got to the barn, they got off their horses. Billy looked at the barn then at his Pa.

"Billy, this was your idea. Go inside and see if you can find a lantern," Pa said.

Billy looked at his Pa for a moment before he looked back at the barn. He reached out and handed the reins of his horse to Donny. Billy walked up to the door to the barn, then looked back at his father. When he saw his father nod his head, and waved for him to go inside, Billy reached down and put his hand on his gun. With his other hand on the barn door, he slowly pulled it open.

Standing just outside the door, Billy looked around. He couldn't see much, but he did see a lantern hanging on a nail just inside, next to the door. He reached inside, took the lantern off the peg and shook it. He stepped back away from the barn and showed the lantern to his father.

"Pa, this here lantern's got oil in it."

"Well, light the darn thin', then go inside and check out the barn."

"Yes, Pa."

Billy lit the lantern then stepped just inside the barn. Standing just inside the barn, he held the lantern up then looked around. The lantern did not give off a lot of light, but Billy was able to see that there were eight stalls in the barn. They all appeared to be empty.

Suddenly, an owl flew down from the rafters. It passed so close to Billy's head that the tip of its wing brushed Billy's face. He ducked almost dropping the lantern. The big bird had scared him.

"Stop foolin' around, Billy. What did ya see in there?" Pa asked.

"I seen an owl. It attacked me and it scared me half to death."

"An owl ain't goin' ta hurt ya none," Donny said.

"How you'd like it if'n a big bird like that hit ya in the face with its wing?"

"You boys stop that. Is that all ya found?" Pa asked.

"No, Pa. It looks like there's some hay in here. If we stay, we can put the horses up here, they'll be in out of the wind."

"Okay," Pa said. "We'll put 'um up in the barn for the night, then we need to get some rest ourselves."

"What about us, Pa? Where we going to sleep?" Billy asked.

"Well, like Donny said. Pick a buildin' and it's all yours."

"We ain't sleepin' in the barn tagether?" Billy asked.

"I ain't sleepin' in no barn," Donny said. "There's a saloon right down the street a little ways. I think I'll be beddin' down there. I might even find a bottle with some whiskey in it."

"I'm goin' ta bed down in the bank," Pa said. "It looked like a pretty solid buildin' to me."

"Ya mean, I gotta sleep in the barn – alone?"

"What? Ya afeared of sleepin' alone," Donny teased with a grin.

"Donny, quit picking on your brother. In the morning, we'll check out the rest of the buildin's ta see if there is anythin' we can use while the horses get some rest. You two get the horses fed, rubbed down and watered."

Donny and Billy walked the horses into the barn, then into the stalls. They got some hay and put it in the stalls for the horses, then unsaddled them. They put the saddles over the heavy boards that made up the stalls. They were so tired, they didn't even notice that the sides of the stalls where higher than most stalls for horses. Donny found a couple of rags hanging on a wall. He took one and began rubbing down the horses.

"Billy, check out in back and see if there's a well or somethin' where we can get water," Pa said.

"Okay, Pa."

Billy went out of the barn. He walked around behind the barn where he found a bucket that was full of water near the edge of the fence to a corral. The bucket had been buried in the dirt with only about six or seven inches of it sticking up above the ground. The bucket was full of water and it was overflowing. It seemed to be bubbling up from the bottom of the bucket. Billy noticed that the water overflowing the sides of the bucket was quickly disappearing in the dry, sandy earth around the outside edge of the bucket. He was so fascinated by what he was seeing that he didn't see the hoof prints around the bucket.

"Hey, Pa. You got to see this." Billy called out.

Billy's father came around the corner of the barn and saw Billy standing near the fence just looking at the ground.

"What ya got, boy?"

"Looky here. There's a bucket that keeps puttin' out water. That's the strangest thin' I ever did see."

Billy's father looked at the bucket, then reached out and hit Billy on the shoulder.

"What ya do that fur?"

"That's a spring. Don't ya know nothin'?"

"I'd seen springs before, but I ain't never seen water run out of a full bucket like that."

"Somebody took a bucket and broke the bottom out of it," Pa explained. "They took the bucket that the bottom was broke out of and put it over the spring, so it could capture the water. It made it easy ta get it so it could be drunk, or used to fill other buckets."

"Well, I'll be darned. That's pretty clever."

"Get some of the water to the horses," Pa said with a discussed look on his face.

Billy looked at his father as if he didn't know how he was going to get it to the horses. If the bottom of the bucket was broken out, how was he going to get any water to the horses.

Pa saw Billy scratching his head as he looked at the spring. It was clear that Billy didn't know how to get the water to the horses from the spring.

"Billy, there's another bucket in the barn. Dip water from this bucket to another bucket and give it to the horses. Didn't your ma teach ya anything?"

"Oh, whatever ya do, don't move that bucket in the ground out of where it is. Don't even touch that bucket. If'n you do, we won't have no water. Ya understand?"

"Yes, Pa." Billy said.

Billy had been so fascinated with the spring that he didn't notice the rather large hoof print in the sand close to the spring. He thought the spring was kind of a neat thing, but his thoughts were interrupted by his Pa.

"Good. Now get them horses water."

"Yes, Pa."

Billy followed his father into the barn. He found another bucket and went back to the spring. Billy carried water into the barn for the horses until they had had their fill.

Once the horses had been taken care of, and bedded down for the night, Billy looked around the barn. He was trying to find a place where he could lay out his bedroll. He found a stall close to the door that had some straw on the floor. He decided he would lay out his bedroll there.

Once he had his bedroll laid out, he looked around the barn. He could hear the wind as it blew around and through the sides of the old barn and nearby buildings. It made strange noises as it whistled around the barn. He looked over and found Pa and Donny standing near the barn door.

"I'm goin' to sleep here in the barn," Billy said.

"Okay. You can keep an eye on the horses. I'm goin' to the saloon," Donny said.

Billy watched as his father and brother left the barn. Billy wasn't sure he liked the idea of sleeping alone in the barn while his brother went to the saloon and his Pa went to the bank to sleep. The thought that he had the horses close by relieved some of his fears of being alone in the barn. He was sure that the horses would warn him if anyone, or anything, tried to cause him trouble.

Billy laid down on his bedroll in the stall that was closest to the barn door. He was only a few feet from the barn door. He laid there for some time just listening to the wind.

The sound of the wind whistling through the cracks in the barn kept Billy from falling asleep, even though he was tired after the long, hard ride. It took him a long time to relax enough to doze off.

Shortly after he dozed off, he was awakened by a strange sound coming from behind the barn. He turned and looked toward the door at the back of the barn. It was open about a foot and a half. His eyes got big when he saw some sort of large animal walk by the door. The bright moonlight cast strange looking shadows as the creature moved slowly past the door.

In the dark, Billy could not see it very well. What he was seeing was more like a shadow moving across the back of the barn. The only thing he seemed to understand was that whatever it was, it was larger than a horse, much larger, yet it didn't make hardly a sound. It scared him so much that he couldn't speak. He didn't dare to move, not that he could have if he wanted to move.

It was just about two minutes before the shadowy figure of the large animal disappeared out of sight. Once it was gone, Billy was able to take a breath somewhere close to normal again. It took him several minutes to gather himself.

Billy continued to listen very carefully. Whatever it was that had walked past the barn, it seemed to be taking its time around the back of the barn near the spring. Billy laid very quiet hoping that the giant creature would go away. It wasn't long before he thought he could hear the creature going away from the barn. It was only a few minutes until he could no longer hear it. The only thing he could hear was the sound of the wind whistling through the cracks in the barn's siding. With the creature finally gone, Billy was able to get at least a little sleep.

When morning came, Billy woke up. He looked around the barn to see if there was anything that didn't belong there. He got up and slowly moved over to the barn door at the back of the barn. With his hand on his gun, he looked out to see if the creature was still around. He didn't see it.

Billy started looking around for some sign of what he thought he saw. He saw nothing, not even the tracks of their horses. The wind had blown all night. The wind had blown the dirt around, and it had covered all the tracks near the back of the barn. He began to think that he had been dreaming, but it sure seemed like he was awake all the time the creature had been behind the barn.

"What ya looking at," Donny asked as he walked up to Billy.

"Nothin'."

"Nothin'? Ya was sure lookin' plenty hard for it to be nothin'. I saw ya lookin' down at the ground as if ya was lookin' for somethin'. Did ya lose somethin'?"

"I weren't lookin' at nothin'."

"What ya boys arguin' about, now?"

"Billy was looking awful hard for somethin' on the ground."

"What was ya looking for, Billy?"

"Nothin'. I weren't looking for nothin'."

"Billy, gather up some wood and make a fire so Donny can fix us somethin' ta eat."

"Yes, Pa."

Billy didn't want to say anything about what he thought he saw last night. He knew that Donny would just make fun of him. Billy wasn't even sure he had really seen anything. He might have just dreamed it, although it sure seemed like it was real to Billy.

Billy went around behind the barn and started gathering some wood to build a fire. As he started to pick up a piece of wood up against the barn, he noticed what looked like the hoof prints in the dirt of some kind of animal. He had seen the hoof prints of many horses. This hoof print was certainly not the hoof print of a horse, or any other kind of animal he had ever seen. It reminded him of the shadow he had seen last night of a large, strange kind of animal. Maybe he hadn't been dreaming, he thought.

"Pa! Pa! Come quick!"

"What ya yelling about?" Pa asked as he came around the corner of the barn with Donny right behind him.

"Looky here," Billy said as he pointed to the hoof print.

"What the heck is that?" Donny asked as he stared at the hoof print.

"Ya got me. I ain't never seen tracks like that before," Pa said.

"It has to be from a pretty good size animal," Donny said.

"I saw the shadow of a very big strange looking animal last night. I thought I was dreamin', but I guess I weren't."

"Ya think that might be the reason this here town was deserted?" Donny asked.

"Could be," Pa said. "Somethin' big enough to make a track like that would be big enough ta scare a lot of people. I think we should get out of here."

Suddenly, Billy's eyes got big as he looked past his pa.

"Pa, ya best turn around very slowly."

Pa looked at Billy. The look on Billy's face was enough to scare anyone. Pa slowly turned around. Standing between the three of them and the door to the barn were seven large camels. Sitting on the backs of the camels were seven men with rifles pointed right at them. Six of the men were soldiers. The seventh was the marshal from Tombstone. He had been following them across the desert.

"Sorry to interrupt your breakfast, but the three of you are under arrest for murdering that bank teller in Tombstone, and for robbing the bank."

Billy, Donny, and their Pa just stood there looking at the camels. They had never seen camels before, and the camels towered over them.

Three of the soldiers got down off their camels, then shackled Billy, Donny and Pa. They led their prisoners to the Dustyville jail, where they locked them up.

"What ya going to do with us," Billy asked.

"We are going to take you back to Tombstone to stand trial for robbery and murder. We'll leave first thing in the morning. It will give your horses a chance to rest a little more before we leave."

"Mr. Marshall, sir. What kind of animals are those you was a ridin'?" Billy asked.

"Those are camels. They live in the desert. These camels belong to the U.S. Army. Camels can travel much further and faster than a horse can in the desert. They can travel for days without water. They are better suited for the desert than horses.

"There is a military outpost not too far from Dustyville that had some camels. I got the Commanding Officer of the Fort to use them to help me catch you. Since I had never ridden a camel before, he sent some of his men who ride camels to come with me to capture you."

After the horses had rested up. The three were taken to the fort where the camels were stationed. From there, the marshal took the three back to Tombstone. They were tried for bank robbery and the coldblooded murder of the bank teller. All three of them were found guilty of the charges and were hung in Tombstone, Arizona.

Historical note: At one time, there were camels used in the southwest desert by the U.S. Army. When they were no longer being used, the camels were simply turned loose. For decades after the Army stopped using camels, there had been reports from time to time from people who claimed they had seen camels in the southwestern deserts of Arizona and New Mexico.

OUT OF THE WILDERNESS

Saul Becker was in his late twenties. He was tall with broad shoulders, dark hair that hung down on his shoulders and a beard that was shaggy. He was dressed in buckskin shirt and pants, and wore a wide brimmed hat that shaded his dark brown eyes. There was an eagle feather stuck in the brim of his hat. Saul wore high top moccasins with a very sharp knife with a four-inch blade in the top of his moccasin on his right leg. On his belt, he had a long sharp knife with a twelve-inch blade, and a .44 caliber Navy Colt that had seen a good deal of action in the years he was in the mountains. He also had a long barrel .50 caliber Sharps rifle tied to the packs on one of the horses.

Saul was a mountain man who had been in the Rocky Mountains for a little over eight years. Other than a couple of mountain men and a few Indians he had become friends with, Saul did his best to avoid anyone who might be a threat to him whenever possible.

The last time he had seen any of the other mountain men was almost four years ago. He had not seen another white man since.

He had spent a good deal of his time hunting for food and for furs that he could trade for things he needed, but he didn't need much. Saul had quickly learned how to find or make those things he needed.

Saul had built a small cabin up against a tall cliff and in an area that was very hard to find. It was hidden by rough terrain and thick forests. The cabin was almost invisible to anyone who might come into the area. Next to the cabin was a cave where he could hide if he needed to, as well as store his furs and pelts he had gathered over the years.

He had one riding horse he had gotten from an Indian who traded it to him for a couple of buffalo hides. Saul also had four pack horses that could carry the fruits of his labor. He had taken the horses from some Indians, who tried to kill him, since they no longer had need of them.

One day, Saul decided it was time for him to take his furs and pelts, and trade them. He also decided that it was time to leave the wilderness and the life of a mountain man. It was a lonely life. Something deep inside his mind, told him it was time to find some other way to make a living, and to meet new people.

Saul packed up all his belongings on his pack horses and set out to make a new life for himself. The pack horses carried pelts from the beaver he trapped, and furs and skins of wolves, buffalo and deer that he had killed. He even had the hide of a mountain lion that he had killed after it injured one of his horses.

Saul Becker had traveled a long way before he came to a dirt road that stretched out across the rolling foothills of the Rocky Mountains. He followed the road across the open prairie until he reached the western side of the Black Hills. He found a long and narrow trail that cut across the southern end of the Black Hills.

He had been travelling for well over a month from the Rocky Mountains on his way to a trading post he knew about on the Missouri River. The trail he was taking took him up on a high hill near the southern end of the Black Hills.

He had just come out of the woods into an area that had once been a small clearing where he had camped with a couple of mountain men when he passed through the area over eight years ago. He suddenly reined up his horse as he looked out over the land in front of him. He looked around unable to believe his eyes.

The clearing was much smaller when he was there last. There had been many more trees then. Now, it looked like most of them had been cut down.

In fact, the last time he was there, it was just a small clearing with a creek running through the forest. It was a place where mountain men would meet every now and then, trade their skins, share stories and do a lot of drinking.

Now there were several buildings where there had not been a single one before. A little ways away, he could see about two dozen tents in neat rows on both sides of the creek that ran through the little valley. There were men squatting down in the water along the banks of the creek. It looked like they were washing pans in the creek, but he soon realized that they were panning for gold in the creek.

Saul looked around at all the activities as he slowly rode into the settlement. He could see that there were only two buildings that looked like they were actually made of wood, but there were a number of tents that had wooden fronts advertising all sort of things and services. Included in the services were one where you could get your clothes washed and one where you could get several different kinds of alcoholic drinks, and one where you could get a woman to spend the night with you.

He could also see a large machine off in the distance. It was out on the edge of the settlement. It looked like it was belching smoke. There was a long line of men in front of it. It looked like they were building a road for the large machine. He was sure it was one of those steam engines that ran on rails back east. He had never seen one, but had heard about them.

Saul rode up in front of one of the wooden buildings, tied his horses to the hitching rail. He swung his leg over his horse and slide off the animal. As soon as his feet hit the ground, he saw a man in a white apron come out of the wooden building in front of him. The sign on the front of the building read, "General Store".

"Well, it looks like you've come a long way," the man said with a smile.

"A bit. Excuse me, but can you tell me where I might find the trading post? I didn't see one on my way here."

"There isn't a trading post in this town."

"Is there somewhere I can trade my furs and pelts?"

"I own the General Store. I've dealt with furs before. I might be able to help you."

"What is the name of this place?" Saul asked as he looked around.

"It's called Willow Crossing. The willow tree it was named after isn't there anymore. Someone cut it down for fire wood," he said with a slight chuckle in his voice.

"Say, how long has it been since you were here last?"

"It's been about eight summers ago. It was just a small clearing back then."

"Eight years? Things have changed a lot since then."

"I can see that," Saul said.

"Willow Crossing is growing fast. We are even getting a railroad through here. People will be able to travel all the way from back east to here in less than four weeks."

Saul wasn't sure he believed the man, but then this little valley had changed a lot since he was here last. It was clear to Saul that he had a lot to learn about this place and what was going on here.

"What's your name, if you don't mind my asking."

"Saul, Saul Becker. What's your name?"

"Will Turner. Let's take a look at those furs. Maybe we can make a deal."

"Sounds good. I was planning on going to the trading post at Fort Pierre."

"Maybe, I can save you the trouble of going so far."

"That sounds good," Saul said.

"Take your furs around back of the store. We'll take a look at them there."

Saul nodded then untied his horses from the hitching rail. He led them around to the back of the store.

Will Turner went through the store and was waiting for Saul when he came around the corner. There was a woman standing next to him.

"Martha, this is Saul Becker. He's a mountain man. He has some furs he might be willing to sell to us.

"It is nice to meet you, Mr. Becker."

"Nice to meet you, Ma'am."

"I'll watch the store while you two talk business," she said.

Saul tipped his hat and watched her as she turned and went back in the store. As soon as she was gone, he turned to Mr. Turner.

"Well, let's see what you have," Will said.

Saul began taking his furs and pelts off his pack horses. He carefully stacked them in piles. As soon as he had them laid out for Mr. Turner to examine, he stepped back and watched as Mr. Turner began looking them over. From what he could see on Mr. Turner's face, he thought they were of good quality.

"You have some mighty fine furs here. I'll give you top dollar for the buffalo and deer hides, and the wolf hides, and this Mountain Lion hide," he said as he pointed at each of the piles of hides.

"What about the beaver pelts?"

"They just aren't worth near as much as they were about two, three years ago. I'll give you the best price I can for them, but the market for beaver pelts hasn't been very good for the past couple years. It seems the folks back east don't want them anymore."

"You mean if I had brought them in three years ago, I'd have gotten a good price for them?"

"Yes, sir. About twice what you can get for them now. Things have changed a lot since you were here last. Just look around."

"Yeah, I noticed some of the changes."

"What do you want to do?" Mr. Turner asked.

Saul looked over the results of his hard work over the past eight years as he rubbed his chin. Mr. Turner seemed like a nice enough fella. One look at the way things had changed since he left, it was not hard for him to believe a lot had changed when it came to the value of pelts and furs, too.

"Well, Mr. Turner, what's your top dollar for everything I got laid out here.

After thinking about it while again looking over what Saul had laid out for him, Mr. Turner looked as Saul.

"I'll give you four hundred dollars in gold coin, and two hundred dollars in store merchandise. You can pick out whatever you want in my store."

Saul looked at the ground for a few minutes before he looked up at Mr. Turner.

"Mr. Turner, I'd been thinking about quitting being a mountain man and getting me a piece of land to farm. Is there any good land around here I could maybe buy with the money?"

"There's a farm of about nine hundred acres owned by a widow lady. It's about three miles or so out of town. She mentioned the other day that she might sell it. You see, she can't get any good man to help her farm it. They all think they are going to get rich panning for gold.

"You might ride out there and talk to her. She might be willing to sell it."

"Are all these men camping along the creek panning for gold?"

"They are, but what little they get ends up in the hands of the saloon owners, if you get what I mean."

"I understand. Mr. Turner, would you mind keeping the furs and skins while I go talk to this widow lady?"

"I'll put them in my building until you have a talk with her," Mr. Turner said with a smile. "Might I make a suggestion before you go see her?"

"Sure. What's on your mind?"

"I don't want to offend you, but it might be a good idea if you get a bath, a haircut and shave before you go see her. A change of clothes might also help," Mr. Turner said.

Saul took a look at himself, then looked at Mr. Turner and smiled.

"You're probably right. Do you have clothes to sell in your store?"

"We do."

"Okay. We have a deal on the price of my furs."

"Okay."

"I would like to buy some clothes out of the two hundred dollars in merchandise you said was part of the deal."

"Martha will be more than happy to help you pick out something suitable for your visit to the widow lady. What would you like me to do with the cash part of our deal?"

"Could you hang onto it until I know if I'm going to buy a piece of land?"

"Yes, I'll do that for you. It will be here whenever you are ready for it," he said with a smile."

"Thanks," Saul said.

Saul went in the store. Mrs. Turner helped him pick out some clothes. As soon as he had new clothes and boots, he went to get a bath, haircut and shave. When he was sure he looked presentable to a widow lady, he took his pack horses to the stable and traded two of his pack horses for a saddle horse, saddle and bridle. He also had his other horses put up at the stable until he knew for sure if he was going to need them.

As soon as he was sure he was ready, he returned to Mr. Turner's General Store. When he walked in the door, Mrs.

Turner was behind the counter. She turned around and just looked at him. She hardly recognized him.

"Do I look okay to visit the widow lady?" Saul asked.

"Mr. Becker, you look just fine," she said then turned and called her husband.

"Will, Mr. Becker is here to see you."

Mr. Turner came in from the back of the store and looked at Saul. He smiled.

"You look very nice, Saul."

"I would like to buy one of those nice saddle rifles and a pistol with a nice holster."

"Pick out the ones you want."

Saul looked over the selection of rifles and pistols. He picked out a Henry repeating rifle and a Colt .45 Peacemaker six shooter with a holster, as well as some ammunition for them. He used his credit with Mr. Turner to pay for them.

"Will, you never told me what the widow lady's name is."

"I guess I didn't. Her name is Sarah Hamilton. She has been a widow for almost two years. Take the road east out of town. It's about three miles from here. You can't miss it. There's a sign over the gate that reads 'Hamilton Ranch'."

"Thank you. I'll go out and pay her a visit."

Saul left the General Store, got on his horse and rode east out of town. As he rode along, he looked over the country. The ground looked like it was good land for farming as well as raising a few cattle.

As he crossed a creek, he noticed that there was a house just about two hundred yards north of the road and close to the creek. In a short time, he came up to a gate along the road. The sign above the gate read, "Hamilton Ranch". He turned and headed toward the house.

As he got closer to the house, he noticed that there was a barn behind the house. There were also several head of cattle grazing in the field to the east of the house.

When he rode up to the house, a woman stepped out on the porch. The first thing he noticed was that the woman was about his age and was very nice looking. He also noticed that she held a rifle loosely in her hands.

Saul rode up to the hitching rail in front of the house. He kept his hands where she could see them easily. He had no idea what she was thinking, but he was sure that she was being very careful. Saul stopped at the hitching rail, but remained in the saddle.

"Good afternoon, ma'am," Saul said.

"What do you want?"

"Are you Mrs. Sarah Hamilton?"

"Yes. What do you want?"

"I'm Saul Becker and I would like to talk to you about your farm. Mr. Will Turner at the General Store told me that you might be looking to sell your farm."

"He did, did he?"

"Yes, ma'am, he did."

"I don't think I have ever seen you before. You aren't from around here, are you?"

"No, ma'am. Up until earlier today, I was in the mountains out west."

"What were you doing there?"

"I guess you would have called me a mountain man. I spent several years hunting and trapping in the Rocky Mountains. I did pretty well, but it is time for a change. Furs don't bring much money anymore. I would like to farm."

"Why haven't you taken up panning for gold? It seems to be what most of the men around here do," she said with a hint of anger in her voice.

"Well, Ma'am. I'm looking to settling down in one place. Farming is something I know how to do. I come from a family of farmers back east. If you're interested in selling your place, I might be interested in buying your farm for a fair price. Can I get down so we can sit down and talk about it?"

She looked at Saul. He seemed to be honest enough. She was sure that Will would not have sent him to see her if he didn't trust him. Besides he was rather good looking and he seemed to be fairly well educated. More important, he seemed to be a straight forward and honest man. He would not say that Will Turner sent him out to see her because he would know that she might check with Will.

"I guess it would be all right. Would you care for a cup of coffee, Mr. Becker?"

"That would be nice, ma'am. Feel free to call me, Saul."

"Okay, Saul."

Saul got down off his horse and tied it to the hitching rail. As he stepped up on the porch, Sarah turned and went into the house. Saul followed her inside.

"You can sit in the parlor while I go to the kitchen and make some coffee."

"If you don't mind, Ma'am, we could sit in the kitchen and talk while you make the coffee. Talking around the kitchen table back on the farm was where we always discussed important things. I'm sure you want to know about me."

Sarah looked at him for a minute and smiled.

"Okay. Right this way."

Saul followed her into the kitchen. He sat down at the table and watched her. Nothing much was said while she made the coffee. He just watched her. Once the coffee was ready, she set a cup of coffee down in front of him, then sat down across the kitchen table with her cup of coffee.

It wasn't long before they were talking more about themselves, mostly about him, than about her farm. Saul made a point of telling her about himself, growing up on a farm back in Iowa as a youngster, then leaving for an adventure into the Rocky Mountains to be a mountain man. He had no problem answering her questions freely, and she had a lot of questions for him.

Sarah felt comfortable with him for some reason, but she couldn't quite figure out why. She found him easy to talk to. She told him about coming to the Dakota Territory from Ohio with her new husband to farm, and how things went well for them over the four years they had together. They had built up the farm from nothing but a piece of land to a well-established farm that provided a reasonably good living for them. Her husband had died only a year and a half ago from a cold that turned into pneumonia.

Sarah had been able to hire a couple of men to help her keep the farm going, but they deserted her when gold was discovered in the creeks in and around the Black Hills. For the past few months, she had been able to keep the farm going, but it was too much for her to do alone.

They talked for several hours, mostly about themselves and a little about the farm. It was getting on toward dinner time. Sarah was the first to realize the lateness of the hour.

"It is almost time for dinner. Would you like to stay and have dinner with me?" Sarah asked. "I don't get much company living out here."

She was hoping he would stay and have dinner with her. She wasn't sure if it was because she was lonely for someone to talk to, and because he was easy to talk to, or if it was because she simply enjoyed his company. She felt that all were good reasons to ask him to stay for dinner.

"I'd be pleased to have dinner with you. Is there something I could do to help?"

It surprised her that he was willing to help her in the kitchen. She wasn't sure how to answer him. None of the men who worked for her ever asked if they could help with a meal. She could see no reason not to let him help her.

"You can set the table, if you like. The dishes are in the cabinet next to the door, and the silverware is in the drawer in the cabinet."

They continued to talk about all sorts of things while Saul set the table and Sarah cooked a meal for them. When the dinner was ready, they sat down and ate.

When dinner was over, Saul stood up and took his dishes over to the dry sink. She looked at him. Her husband had never done that simple thing to help her in the kitchen.

"Is there something that I can do for you before I go back to town?" Saul asked.

She looked at him, but didn't say anything. The look on her face confused Saul. He wondered what he had said.

"I can take care of your horses before I go," he suggested.

"That would be nice of you. Thank you."

Saul left the house and walked out to the barn. He took the horses from the corral and led them one at a time into the barn. He made sure that each of them had water and hay before he went back to the house.

"Are you finished already?" Sarah asked when he came back into the house.

"Yes, ma'am. They are all fed and watered. They are good solid stock. I want to thank you for dinner, but I should be heading back to town."

"Saul, please don't call me ma'am. I think you can call me, Sarah."

"Okay, Sarah."

"Won't you stay long enough to have a cup of coffee before you leave?"

Saul got the feeling that she didn't want him to leave. He was sure that she was lonely, spending day after day doing the work that needed to be done around the farm all by herself.

"Yes, Sarah. That would be nice. I'll wash up a bit."

Saul followed her back into the house. He went out to the back porch to the wash basin. He washed up a little then returned to the kitchen.

"Coffee is ready. Please sit down."

Saul sat down at the kitchen table. They talked about the farm for a little while. Saul noticed it was getting rather late. He didn't really want to leave. He found Sarah to be very nice to talk to, and she was a good cook. It had been a long time since he had anyone cook for him. She was also very nice looking. He was sure that she was something special.

"I really should be going," Saul said reluctantly.

He drank down the last of his coffee, set the cup on the table and stood up. Saul noticed the look on her face as she stood up. He turned and walked to the front door.

Sarah followed him to the door, all the time trying to think of some way to get him to stay. She quietly chastised herself for wishing he would stay, but she couldn't help how she was feeling. She had never felt that way about any other man since her husband had died.

As soon as Saul stepped off the front porch, he turned to thank her for the dinner and the conversation. He was also going to ask her if he could call on her again. When he looked at her, he suddenly was hoping that she would ask him to stay. It was nothing she said, but maybe it was the look on her face that gave him the idea that she didn't want him to leave any more than he wanted to leave.

"Saul, it is very dark out tonight, and there is no moonlight to help show you the way. I don't think it would be safe for you to be riding all the way back to town in the dark, especially since you do not know the area very well."

She didn't come right out and ask him to stay, but it was clear that she didn't want him to leave.

"I guess you are right. Where did the hired men sleep when they were working here?"

"They slept in the barn and ate on the back porch."

"I could sleep in the barn, if you don't mind?"

"Saul, I would like you to put your horse up in the barn, then come in the house to sleep."

"If I come in the house, people might talk. I wouldn't want that to happen to you."

"I don't care what they think or say about me. I want you to stay here, with me," she blurted out.

She was a little surprised at what she had said, but she was not embarrassed about it.

"Are you sure?" Saul asked.

"Yes," she said. "I want you to stay here, with me."

"If I stay the night with you, I stay for keeps," Saul said, not sure what she would think of that comment.

She looked at Saul for a minute, then began to smile.

"I want you to stay. I know more about you in just one evening than I knew about my husband in all the years we were married."

"I'll go put my horse up."

"I'll be waiting for you," she said with a smile.

Saul and Sarah spent the night together, and the days and nights that followed. After several days, Saul went into Willow Crossing and collected his money from Will Turner. He bought some more clothes and other things that he would need, as well as some supplies for the farm using money from his account with Will Turner. He also got the horses he had left with the blacksmith, then returned to the ranch.

It was about six weeks before the circuit preacher came to Willow Crossing. Sarah and Saul got married in the yard behind the General Store with Will and Martha standing up for them.

They used the money Saul had earned as a mountain man to buy up more land around the farm and turned the farm into a ranch. They changed the sign above the main gate to read, "Becker Ranch".

Over the years, they had three children, two boys and a girl. They bought up more land around the farm and turned it into a large ranch where, as the story goes, they lived happily ever after.

MARSHAL SAM PHILLIPS

A man came riding into the small Black Hills town of Custer. His horse was a tall, strong looking animal that was covered with the dust and dirt of a horse that had traveled a long distance in a short time with very little rest.

On the horse's back, in a plain black saddle, was a tall man with broad shoulders, narrow waist, and a six-gun strapped down to his leg. The man rode the horse with an air of confidence. He wore a wide brimmed hat that shaded his eyes. On his shirt was the silver badge of a Territorial Marshal. Everyone took notice of him as his horse plodded along the street.

The marshal rode up in front of the Sheriff's Office and sat in the saddle as he looked up and down the main street of the town. He had been in this town a number of times over the past few years. It was like a lot of the small towns on the frontier and in the Black Hills. It had a general store, a bank, livery stable, blacksmith's shop and a couple of saloons. It also had a couple of hotels. There were also several small shops mixed in among the other businesses.

The man reached down and patted the horse on its neck, then stepped out of the saddle. He led his horse to the watering trough next to the hitching rail, then stood next to the horse while it drank.

As soon as the horse had finished drinking, he tied it to the hitching rail and patted it on the neck again. With his horse taken care of, at least for the moment, he took his rifle from the saddle scabbard, turned and stepped up on the boardwalk. He looked around again, then reached out, opened the door to the sheriff's office and walked inside.

Sheriff Walter Filmore was sitting at his desk. He looked up and began to smile.

"Well, I'll be. If it isn't Marshal Sam Phillips. I haven't seen you for a long time," the sheriff said as he stood up.

"It's good to see you, too," the marshal said as he reached across the desk and shook hands with the sheriff.

"Sit down. What brings you all the way out here?"

Marshal Phillips leaned his rifle against the wall in a corner, then sat down in front of the sheriff's desk.

"I'm after three men who held up the stagecoach just outside Silver City late yesterday afternoon. They killed two passengers and the driver. They opened the strong box and relieved it of about six thousand dollars worth of gold."

"What makes you think they came this way?"

"The stagecoach driver lived long enough to tell me who the man was who shot him. He didn't live long enough to tell me who the others were."

"Who was the one he told you about?"

"You won't believe me."

"Who was it? I'll believe you."

Sheriff Filmore leaned forward on his desk waiting for the marshal to tell him who had killed the passengers and driver of the stagecoach.

"It was Brother Paul from your church right here in Custer."

"You're kidding?"

"I told you, you wouldn't believe me."

"You're sure that's what he said?"

"Not directly."

"What do you mean, 'not directly'?" the sheriff asked.

"What he did was describe the man who shot him. He said he was wearing a brown loose-fitting robe with a hood that shaded most of the man's face. He said the man looked just like Brother Paul. He said the man was about Brother Paul's height and build. He even said that he saw the scar on his cheek. I understand that Brother Paul has a scar on his cheek."

"He does, but it is a small one and difficult to see. I still find it hard to believe," Sheriff Filmore said, shaking his head. "Do you think he was telling you what he thought he saw, but it was not really what he saw. The mind can play tricks on a man when he's in a lot of pain, or is dying, ya know?"

"Yes, I do know. I also know that I need to have a talk with Brother Paul. I want to know where he was at the time of the robbery of the stagecoach."

"By the way, I'm interested in knowing how is it you got to Silver City so soon after the stagecoach was held up?" the sheriff asked.

"I was in Silver City on another matter when the stagecoach arrived late last evening. The driver managed to get the stagecoach into Silver City. A couple of prospectors were able to grab the horses to stop the stagecoach.

"The two passengers were dead in the stagecoach, but the driver was still alive. He lived long enough to tell me that there were three man, and described the one who shot him. He wasn't able to describe the other two involved in the robbery. Since it was almost dark when the stagecoach got into Silver City, there wasn't much I could do until this morning.

"I left Silver City early this morning and made a brief stop in Hill City. I talked to the local blacksmith. He said that he saw Brother Paul as he rode through town with two other men. He also said they were headed toward Custer. I didn't stop to rest. I rode straight on to here."

"What's your plan?" Sheriff Filmore asked.

"As soon as I get my horse taken care of, get something to eat and cleaned up a bit; I plan to make a call on Brother Paul. I'm hoping he will tell me who the other two men were who robbed the stagecoach. He still lives in the church, doesn't he?"

"Yes. He still lives there. Do you really think Brother Paul is involved in the killing of those people and the driver?"

"I don't know, but I'm going to talk to him about it. The description I got from the stagecoach driver is all I have to go on. I wouldn't be doing my job if I don't at least talk to Brother Paul."

"I guess you're right. Would it be okay with you if I join you when you're ready to talk to him? I'd like to hear what he has to say."

"Sure. I don't mind. I'll meet you back here in about an hour or so. By the way, I don't want you to say a word to anyone, and don't you go talking to Brother Paul without me," Marshal Phillips said.

"I'll keep quiet. I won't talk to him or anyone else."

Marshal Phillips nodded that he heard him, then left the sheriff's office. He walked his horse down to the Blacksmith Shop and stable. He paid the blacksmith to take care of his horse. He wanted the horse rubbed down good, fed well, then put in a stall to rest.

When he was finished there, he went to the hotel where he got a bath, a shave and a change of clothes. As soon as he was ready, he walked down the street to a café where he got a good meal for himself.

When Marshal Phillips stepped out of the café, he looked up and down the street. Suddenly his eyes caught sight of Brother Paul, or at least it looked like Brother Paul walking down the street. It was hard to tell because his face was covered by the hood on the brown woolen robe he was wearing.

Marshal Phillips looked him over very carefully. The one thing he noticed was that Bother Paul was wearing cowboy boots under his brown hooded robe that didn't quite cover the boots as he walked. The marshal also noticed a bulge just below the rope around his waist as if he had a gun under his robe.

Marshal Phillips had only seen Brother Paul a couple of times, and both times were in Custer. He had never seen Brother Paul wearing cowboy boots, he always wore sandals.

He had never noticed that Brother Paul ever carried anything that would cause a bulge in his robe. The bulge under Brother Paul's robe looked like he might be carrying a gun. What would Brother Paul need a gun for, especially when it would be difficult to get it out from under the robe in a hurry if he did have need of it, Marshal Phillips wondered?

When talking to people about Brother Paul in the past, he had heard that Brother Paul was a peaceful man, and not prone to violence of any kind. No one Marshal Phillips had ever talked to had seen him with a weapon of any kind, gun or knife. Nor had anyone ever seen him get even a little angry.

Marshal Phillips was beginning to think that maybe it wasn't Brother Paul he was watching walk along the boardwalk on the other side of the street. He decided that he would follow him to see where he was going.

Marshal Phillips casually walked across the street and stepped up on the boardwalk. He followed the man at a distance. It wasn't long before the man turned around and looked his way.

The marshal turned and walked into a saddle shop he was just about to walk by. As soon as he was inside the shop, he went to the window and peeked out. He saw the man look around as if to see if anyone was watching him. The man then turned and went between a saloon and the freight station.

Marshal Phillips knew that the church was on the other side of the street, and in the wrong direction from where the man was going. He decided not to pursue the man, but go get the sheriff instead. As soon as the man disappeared between the buildings, he stepped out of the saddle shop and began walking back toward the sheriff's office.

Marshal Phillips walked into the sheriff's office. He pulled up a chair and sat down.

"You look better," Sheriff Filmore said.

"I feel better, too. Say, have you ever noticed Brother Paul wear anything other than sandals?"

"No. He always wears sandals. He even wears them in the winter. I don't think he even has a pair of boots. Why?"

"I saw someone who looked like Brother Paul. The man was built like Brother Paul, but he was wearing cowboy boots under his robe. I could see them as he walked. He also had a bulge in his robe on the right side, just about where a man would have a gun in a holster."

"What would Brother Paul want with a gun?"

"That's a good question. I even asked myself that very question. I don't think it was Brother Paul," Marshal Philips said.

"Any idea who it might be?"

"No, but I plan to find out. It might be the man the stagecoach driver saw."

"It doesn't make sense to dress up like a brother, especially like Brother Paul," the sheriff said."

"I think it makes perfect sense if you want to hide your identity, and shift the blame for something you did onto someone who people would never suspect of doing it."

"But to make it look like Brother Paul robbed a stagecoach and killed three people? People would find that hard to believe," the sheriff said shaking his head.

"They sure would. But maybe that was what they wanted. To confuse people and have them looking in the wrong direction."

"What's your next move?" the sheriff asked.

"I'm going to follow his tracks. The last time I saw him, he was going between the saloon and the freight station. I should be able to pick up his tracks there."

"That's the wrong way to get to the church."

"Yeah, I know."

"What do you want me to do?" the sheriff asked.

"I want you to go to the stable and get a horse ready to ride. My horse is about done in. He's not ready for any kind of a chase, if it comes to that. We need to be ready for anything."

"I'll pick out a good sturdy horse for you, and one for myself" the sheriff assured him.

"Thanks. I'll head over to where I saw the man last. Join me over at the freight station as soon as you can."

Marshal Phillips left the sheriff's office and began walking toward where he had last seen the man in the brown hooded robe. He walked up to the front of the saloon, then moved to the corner. He carefully peeked around the corner and looked down between the buildings. There was no one there.

He drew his gun then stepped around the corner. As he walked slowly between the buildings, he glanced down at the ground. He could see footprints made by the man who was wearing the robe. He had walked toward the back of the building. The marshal slowly followed the footprints, being very careful not to be surprised.

When he got to the back corner of the saloon, he carefully looked around the corner. There was a small cabin only about twenty-five feet behind the saloon.

The cabin had two small windows and a door on the front of it. There were three horses tied to the hitching rail in front of the cabin. They were saddled and ready to ride. It looked like whoever owned the horses was getting ready to leave.

Marshal Phillips was sure he had found the three who had robbed the stagecoach and killed the passengers and driver. The questions that came to mind were all three of the men in the cabin or were there more than just the three?

Just as the marshal turned back away from the corner of the saloon to think about how he was going to get the three out of the cabin, a shot rang out. A bullet hit the corner of the saloon scattering several pieces of wood from the building. It missed the marshal by inches.

Marshal Phillips ducked down. He moved to the edge of the saloon, then quickly fired three shots at the cabin, then ducked back. His three shots were quickly responded to by several shots from the cabin, several of them hitting the corner of the saloon.

For the next few minutes several shots were exchanged between the marshal and the men in the cabin. After one volley of shots, the marshal thought he heard a cry of pain come from the cabin. He was sure he had hit one the men in the cabin. The only problem was, he had no idea if the injured man was out of the fight or not.

There was several minutes of quiet. It was suddenly broken by one of the men in the cabin.

"Listen carefully, Sheriff. You will back off and let us go or we will kill Brother Paul."

By this time the sheriff had come to the marshal's aid.

"What do we do? I don't want to have Brother Paul killed," the sheriff said.

"I don't think it is Brother Paul."

"Are you willing to take the chance that Brother Paul is not in that cabin?"

There was a long pause while Marshal Phillips thought about it. He was almost sure it wasn't Brother Paul, but not a hundred percent sure.

"Well, what's it going to be?" someone in the cabin yelled, disturbing the marshal's thoughts.

"I'm thinking."

"You better think fast. We ain't got all day."

"Is there any way out of that cabin other than the front door?" Marshal Phillips asked the sheriff.

"No. The only windows and door are in the front. What's on your mind?"

"Do you know what's in the cabin?"

"Nothing, except for a small bed in the corner, a table with two chairs in the room, and what those three might have taken in there. No one has lived in it for several years."

"The smoke stack, is there a stove at the bottom of it?"

"Yeah. There's a cast iron pot belly stove. Why?"

"Where is the stove. Is it close to the bed?"

"If I remember correctly, it's in the corner across the room from the bed. But that don't mean they didn't move the bed."

"Good. I want you to get about two-inches from a stick of dynamite and a fuse. Get it as quickly as you can and bring it back here."

The sheriff just looked at him for a few seconds, then began to smile. Realizing what the marshal had in mind, he turned and ran back to the street.

Sheriff Filmore hurried down the street to the General Store. He entered the store and told the owner he wanted him to cut two-inches off the end of a stick of dynamite.

"What you want that for?"

"I don't have time to discuss it with you, just get it, now!"

The store owner took a stick of dynamite and cut two-inches off it. He handed it to the sheriff. The sheriff cut a short piece of fuse off the cord of it, then ran out the door.

The owner of the store just stood there and watched as the sheriff ran out of the store. He was wondering what had just happened.

The sheriff returned to where Marshal Phillips was watching the cabin. He showed the marshal the piece of dynamite and the fuse.

"Can you get around behind the cabin without being seen?" the marshal asked.

"Yeah, sure."

"Okay. I want you to get around behind the cabin, climb up in that tree at the back corner of the cabin. From there you should be able to reach the smoke stack without walking on the roof. When you are ready, light the fuse and drop the dynamite down the stove pipe. Be sure to get away from the stove pipe before the dynamite goes off. A lot of the force of that dynamite will come back up the stove pipe. I'll keep them busy while you do it."

"What about Brother Paul. He might be in that cabin."

"That little bit of dynamite inside that cast iron stove shouldn't do a lot of damage to the inside of the cabin. If they have Brother Paul in there, he is probably tied to the bed. That little bit of dynamite will probably make it hard for anyone in there to hear for awhile after it goes off. It might cause a few minor injuries, but it is unlikely that it will kill anybody. As soon as it goes off, I'll rush the door."

"I sure hope you know what you are doing," Sheriff Filmore said.

"So do I, now get going. They are probably getting a little nervous and might do something stupid."

"Right."

Marshal Phillips watched as the sheriff ran back toward the front of the saloon. Once he was out of sight, the marshal turned back and looked around the corner toward the cabin.

"Well," the man in the cabin yelled.

"Hold your horses. I'm thinking."

"I'm tired of waiting. You've got just five minutes and then I'm going to kill Brother Paul."

Marshal Phillips didn't respond. He kept watch of the cabin. It wasn't long before he saw Sheriff Filmore climbing the tree at the far corner of the cabin.

As soon as the sheriff looked like he was ready to light the fuse on the dynamite. The marshal nodded that he was ready. The sheriff lit a match and touched it to the fuse. He then held the dynamite over the stove pipe, then dropped it down the pipe. The sheriff quickly scrambled down the tree to the ground.

All of a sudden there was a loud bang and smoke and soot flew out the end of the stove pipe, and one of the windows in the cabin blew out.

Marshal Phillips quickly ran to the door of the cabin and kicked it in. The first man he saw as he came charging into the cabin, swung around with a gun in his hand. The marshal shot him.

The second man was kneeling on the floor with his hands over his ears. He looked like he was in pain, but he sat there looking dumbfounded at the marshal. The third man was lying on the floor with blood on his chest. He was dead from one of the exchanges of gunfire before the dynamite went off.

Over in the corner, tied to the bed was Brother Paul in his underwear. Marshal Phillips walked over to him and cut him loose.

"You all right, Brother Paul?"

"Yes, I think so."

"Let's get you out of here."

The sheriff came into the cabin. He went right to Brother Paul. While the marshal took charge of the one prisoner that was alive, the sheriff helped Brother Paul get into his robe, then led him out of the cabin.

It wasn't long before some of the people of Custer came running to see what had exploded. A few of the onlookers took the two dead men to boot hill where they were buried. The one remaining killer was jailed awaiting trial for robbery and murder.

As for Brother Paul, he was just grateful to be alive. He did have a little trouble hearing for awhile, but recovered most of his hearing.

Marshal Phillips spent a couple of days filling out his report about what had happened, and spending some time resting while he waited for the judge to come and hold the trial of the one killer still alive.

He was tried about a week later and found guilty of murder and robbery. He was hung two days later.

As soon as the trial was over, and the verdict was to hang the last one had been carried out by Sheriff Filmore; Marshal Sam Phillips said goodbye to the sheriff and Brother Paul.

It was time for the marshal to head north to check out a complaint about cattle rustlers operating near Spearfish.

When morning came, Marshal Phillips had a good meal, then went to the blacksmith's shop and got his horse. He rode out of town. He headed north toward Spearfish to hunt down the cattle rustlers.

IN A STRANGE LAND

It was a quiet early fall afternoon in Custer, South Dakota, when the stagecoach from Chadron, Nebraska, pulled up in front of the Kleeman House. The driver set the brake, then tied the reins to the brake handle. He climbed down off the stagecoach and walked to the door of the stagecoach and opened it. He reached out his hand to help a young woman out of the stagecoach. She took his hand and stepped to the ground then stepped up on the boardwalk.

The woman's dress was a fairly simple dress by Chicago's standards, but was quite fashionable in western towns like Custer. It was blue with white lace around the neck line, and several petticoats under the full skirt that almost touched the ground. She also wore a sunbonnet that matched the dress.

"This is the Kleeman House, ma'am," the driver said. "I believe you said this was where you are to meet Mr. Thornton."

"Yes, it is." she said.

The woman looked around, but didn't see Mr. Thornton.

"I'll get your bags," the driver said, interrupting her thoughts.

"Oh, yes. Thank you."

The driver retrieved the woman's carpet bag and a suitcase from the top of the stagecoach. He set them on the boardwalk in front of the Kleeman House.

"There you go, ma'am."

"Thank you," she replied.

"Good luck," the drive said then turned to the stagecoach.

The young woman stood on the boardwalk and watched as the stagecoach driver climbed back up on the seat, then called out to the horses. The horses lunged forward and the stagecoach moved forward. The stagecoach was on its way to the next stop.

She didn't know how she felt as she watched the stagecoach turn a corner and disappear from sight. It was as if everything she knew was suddenly leaving with the stagecoach.

The words of the driver gave her cause to think. What did he mean by "good luck"? she wondered. Was it a warning, or just something he said to everyone he dropped off along his route?

She suddenly felt as if she was all alone in a strange land. The small western town of Custer was certainly nothing like Chicago.

Once she was across the Mississippi River on her way to Custer, everything seemed to change. It was as if she had crossed into a completely different world. Little did she know that the frontier west of the Mississippi and Missouri Rivers was a completely different world from the typical farm land of Illinois.

The young woman stood on the boardwalk and looked around. There was nothing familiar to her, but then she had never been this far west in her life. Not only was this place unfamiliar to her, she did not see the man who had written to her for the past year; and she had come all this way to marry. Not seeing him made her feel very much alone. It also caused her to have second thoughts about coming out west. Had she come all this way only to be left on her own? Had he decided that he didn't want to marry her, and instead of telling her, he just didn't show up? His letters did not make her think that he would do such a thing. Yet, where was he?

Get those thoughts out of your head, she thought. He had written in more than one of his letters to her that he could hardly wait to see her. There had to be a good reason that he was not here to greet her, she just knew it. No one would be that cruel.

She turned and looked up at the Kleeman House. It was the place where he was to meet her. Not knowing what else to do, she went into the Kleeman House to get out of the hot sun. Once inside, she set her bags on the floor next to a chair, and looked around the hotel. She was sure this was the place he had written about in his last letter telling her where he would meet her.

Over next to the front windows of the hotel were several chairs where she could sit. She would be able to look out onto the street from there. She picked up her carpet bag and suitcase and walked over to a chair near one of the windows. She set her carpet bag and suitcase next to the chair, then sat down to wait.

The clerk had seen her sit down by the window. He would glance over at her from time to time. He had no idea who the woman was, or why she was there. After seeing her sitting in the lobby of the hotel for almost an hour, the clerk decided he should probably find out who she was, and what she was doing there. He moved out from behind the counter and walked over to the young woman.

"Excuse me ma'am, may I help you?"

"No. I'm waiting for Mr. Ralph Thornton. He said he would meet me here."

"Oh. You must be Miss Emma Wilson?"

"Yes. Do you know Ralph?"

"Yes, of course. Mr. Thornton reserved a room for you here. Would you like to go to your room while you wait for him?"

"No, thank you. I'm fine. I think I will wait for him here, if you don't mind," she said with a slight smile.

"I don't mind at all. In that case, is there anything I can get you while you wait?"

"No, thank you. I'm fine."

"If you need anything, please feel free to let me know."

"I will."

The clerk nodded politely, turned and went back behind the counter. He still looked over at her from time to time.

Emma sat quietly looking toward the door in anticipation of seeing Ralph come through the door at any minute. When he didn't show up, she began to wonder what happened. Was he injured on his way in from his ranch? Did he decide it would be a mistake to marry her?

She could think of a lot of reasons for him not showing up, and none of them were good. The one that kept running through her head was that he found someone here to marry, or he just didn't want her anymore. She felt like crying, but what good would it do.

She again chastised herself for thinking that he had decided not to marry her. The more she thought about it, the more she realized that she was having those same feelings she had had when she was left at the orphanage by her uncle after her parents died. She felt unwanted, almost as if she had been thrown away because she was unworthy of being loved.

Time passed by rather slowly for Emma. She couldn't understand why Ralph didn't show up. She was also beginning to feel hungry. She still had a little money left from what Ralph had sent her for her trip from Chicago to Custer. A look at the clock on the wall showed her that she had been there for almost five hours. She could not understand what was keeping him. With nothing else to do, she decided that she would get something to eat. She got up and walked over to the counter.

"Excuse me, sir, but could you tell where I might get something to eat."

"Yes, ma'am. There are several saloons that offer meals, but the best place to get a good meal would be at Martha's Café. It is right down the street. Go out the door and turn to your right. It's about half way down the next block."

"Thank you."

"If you would like, I will put your carpet bag and suitcase in your room for you. Mr. Thornton has already paid for the room for two nights."

"Thank you. That would be very nice of you."

"You're welcome."

Emma left the hotel and walked down the street to the café. She sat down at a table near the window so she could watch for Ralph.

As she looked out the window, her thoughts turned to what the clerk had said. Ralph had paid for a room for two nights. Did he pay for two nights in case he was unable to get there by the time she was to arrive? That thought made her feel at least a little better. Maybe he got delayed, but he would be there soon, she thought.

As soon as she had finished her dinner, she returned to the Kleeman House. Emma went directly to the counter.

"Excuse me, sir. Has Mr. Thornton come here?"

"I'm sorry, but I have not seen him yet."

"Thank you. I think I would like to go to my room."

"Yes, ma'am."

The clerk turned around, got the key to her room, then handed it to her. She took the key and went to her room. Once inside the room, she just sat down on the bed and stared at the mirror.

"What am I to do if he doesn't show up?" she asked herself.

The sound of her own voice frightened her a little. She had not thought that she might have to look for a way to make a living if he didn't show up.

Emma could no longer help herself. She laid down on the bed and broke down and cried. She had never been so scared. Emma didn't have enough money to stay here longer than the time the room had already been paid for, nor did she have enough money to go back east. She also knew that she didn't have anything to go back to. What was she to do if Ralph didn't show up?

Finally, sleep came and relieved her of her problem for at least a little while. The long trip by trains and then the stagecoaches had been exhausting, which helped her sleep.

Emma woke early, but she was still feeling tired. She sat up on the edge of the bed and looked around the room. She would have to start thinking about what she was going to do if Ralph didn't show up today, or tomorrow at the latest. Not knowing where he was or why he was going to be late, did nothing to ease her fears of being left alone. It was the same kind of fear she had felt when she was sent away from the orphanage when she was just sixteen.

That time she had no place to go, but she met a lady who would take her in. It was Mrs. McDonald who introduced her to the idea of being a mail-order bride. She was also the one who helped her pick out the name of someone to write to out in the west. That name was Ralph Thornton. She wrote to him, and he responded.

They had written back and forth for a little over a year when he sent her a letter asking her if she would marry him. When she wrote back that she would, he sent her the money to make the trip. She enjoyed getting letters from him. With that thought in mind, she could not believe that he didn't want her.

Her thoughts quickly turned back to what was she to do if he didn't come for her soon. She had only a little money, and no place to stay after tomorrow night.

Emma knew her mind was running around in circles. She had to clear her mind and think of something else. She decided that she might have to think of a way to make a living for herself. Emma quickly thought that she should make a mental list of those things she knew how to do, if for no other reason than to be prepared for what might happen if Ralph didn't marry her, or if something happened to him that made it impossible for him to get to her.

The first thing she thought of was that she had learned to cook for the kids and the few adults at the orphanage, so she was skilled at cooking for a large number of people. Maybe, she could get a job as a cook at a café, or at a large ranch that needed a cook to feed the cowboys.

She had learned how to sew. She had even made clothes for the children and for herself. Maybe she could make money by sewing for others. She knew of people who did that sort of work. She remembered that they made good money, but that was in Chicago where there were a lot of women who wanted someone to make dresses for them. She had no idea how well that kind of work would go here.

Emma had also taught the young children at the orphanage reading, writing, and arithmetic. She had not been formally trained as a teacher, but she knew how to teach young children, and how to maintain order in the classroom. It didn't hurt that she had been lucky enough to have had some guidance in her young life on teaching, although no actual schooling. She could certainly teach first through fifth grades. Most of the people she had known had only a fifth-grade education.

"A teacher," she said excitedly. "I would like to be a teacher."

Emma suddenly realized that she didn't know if the town even had a school. "If they don't have a school, maybe I could find a small building and start a school," she said to herself. Certainly, the people of Custer would want to educate their children, she thought.

Emma's thoughts again turned to Ralph. Why had he not been there to meet her? Where was he? He had to know that she was coming. She had sent him a letter telling him her plans. The thought that maybe he didn't get her letter crossed her mind. She tried to clear her mind and focus on her immediate needs.

It was time for Emma to go get some breakfast. She decided that if Ralph didn't show up by the time she finished her breakfast, she would start looking into forming a school if the town didn't have one. She smiled at the thought that the people who would most likely want to see their children be educated, were the mothers of the children. If she didn't get a good response from any of the business people in town, she would present her idea to the mothers in Custer. With the thought of being able to take care of herself if Ralph didn't come for her, she felt that she was ready to face the world.

Emma washed her face, and straighten her clothes in the hope of looking presentable. As soon as she was ready, she walked down the stairs. She went to the counter to talk to the clerk.

"Excuse me, sir."

"Yes. What is it I can do for you, Miss Wilson?"

"Have you heard from Mr. Thornton?"

"No, I'm sorry. It's not like him not to keep appointments. I'm sure he will be here soon."

"I'm sure. I'm going to go for breakfast at Martha's Cafe. If he should come by, please tell him where I will be."

"Yes, ma'am. I will do that."

"Thank you."

Emma left the Kleeman House and walked down the street to Martha's Café. She entered the café and found a place to sit. A woman came over to her table to find out what she would like for breakfast.

"What would you like, ma'am?"

"I would like two eggs, two flapjacks and black coffee. I would also like to ask you a question."

"Sure. What would you like to know?" the waitress asked.

"Do you have a school in this town?"

"We do, but the school teacher got married to a big rancher and left."

"So, you don't have a teacher now? Is that correct?"

"Right, we don't have a teacher now. They're supposed to be looking for one, but they haven't gotten any responses."

"Who would I have to talk to about the teaching position?"

"You are a teacher?"

"I have taught children at an orphanage back east."

"Mr. Briggs at the bank is the one who is supposed to be trying to get a teacher for our school."

"What do you mean by 'supposed to'?"

"I mean he doesn't seem to be trying very hard."

"I guess I will have to go talk to him after my breakfast."

"I'll tell some of the women that you are a teacher. Maybe it will help you get the job if the women of this town put a little pressure on Mr. Briggs," she said with a smile.

"Thank you. By the way, do you know Ralph Thornton?"

"Sure. He works on a ranch out west of town."

"He doesn't own a ranch?"

"I don't think so. I know he has been talking about getting a ranch, and that he has been looking at one that has been for sale for some time. The last time I talked to him, he was getting ready to close the deal on it."

"When was the last time you talked to him?"

"About four or five days ago. He came in for breakfast. He was excited about someone coming on the stagecoach."

"Do you know where the ranch is?"

"No, but I'm sure the sheriff would know where it is."

"Thank you," Emma said.

"Say, are you the mail-order bride he has been talking about?"

Having no idea who Ralph might have talked to about her, she was surprised at the waitress's comment. She wasn't sure what to say.

"It's all right, Honey. A lot of people know he was writing to a woman back east. From what Ralph said, he wasn't expecting you until next week."

"Oh my," Emma said with a shocked look on her face.

"What's the matter?"

"I thought he stood me up, that he didn't really want me."

"Oh, no. You are all he talks about. Ralph is not the type of man who would do something like that to someone. He's a good man, and a hard worker," the waitress said.

"Do you know where I can find him? I need to let him know I'm here."

"Like I said, I don't know where he is, but the sheriff might know."

"Where is the sheriff's office?"

"It's across the street and down the street about two blocks."

"I'm going down there."

"You should probably have breakfast first."

"Oh, yes," she said with a smile.

"I'll get it for you," the young waitress said.

Emma leaned back in the chair and looked out the window. She was chastising herself for all the thoughts she had about Ralph not wanting her, and for not being there to meet her at the stagecoach.

After she finished her breakfast, she stepped out on the boardwalk and looked up and down the street. She saw the sign for the Sheriff's Office just as a young man came riding into town.

The young man reined up in front of the Sheriff's Office. When he stepped out of the saddle, he turned and looked up the street. He stopped suddenly when he saw Emma. When she looked his way, he began to smile.

Emma saw him at the same time. She smiled at him from across the street. Ralph ran across the street and stopped in front of her. He wanted to take her in his arms, but he wasn't sure how she would feel about being kissed on the main street of Custer where everyone could see them.

"Hi," he said shyly. "You are more beautiful than your picture."

"Hi. I got here a little early."

"I know. If I had known you were going to get here early, I would have been here to meet you."

"Is there some place where we can go to talk," Emma asked.

"Why don't we go to your room at the Kleeman House? We could talk in private there."

"Yes. That would be good."

Emma turned in the direction of the Kleeman House. Ralph quickly walked up beside her and took hold of her hand. She turned her head, looked up at him and smiled. The act of taking her hand let Emma know that he really did want her.

They went into the Kleeman House and up to Emma's room. Once inside the room, Ralph took her in his arms. She went willingly.

"I'm sorry I was not here to meet you at the stagecoach. I didn't think you would be here until next week."

"Then why did you reserve a room for this week for me?"

"Well, I didn't really reserve a room for you at any given time. I just reserved a room for when you got here in case I couldn't be here at the time you arrive."

"Oh."

Emma sat down on the edge of the bed while Ralph sat on the only chair in the room. There was a long silence between them before Ralph spoke.

"Emma, I'm sorry, ah, I don't have a ranch."

He looked at her hoping she would not be disappointed with him.

"That's okay."

"I had an agreement with a man that owns a small ranch east of town. I got the money together to buy it, but he backed out at the last minute."

"It's okay. We can work something out. Maybe we can find another ranch for sale and buy it."

"I have been looking for one, but there just aren't any right now."

"Maybe we could find some other type of work until we find a ranch. I'm pretty sure that I can get a job as a teacher."

"How would you feel if you were married to a shop owner?"

"It wouldn't matter what you do as long as it is legal, and we are together," Emma said.

"Back where I came from, my father taught me to work with leather. I can make a lot of things out of leather. He even taught me to make saddles," he said with a hint of pride in his voice."

"What sort of things can you make from leather?"

"I can make fancy tooled leather things like belts, harnesses, saddle bags, holsters and even leather purses."

"It sounds to me that you like working with leather. Do you?"

Ralph thought for a minute, then smiled. He was beginning to understand what she was getting at.

"How would you like to be married to a shopkeeper, a shopkeeper who makes things out of leather, and sells them to people?"

"I came out her to marry you. You said you had a ranch, which you did until the man backed out. If you would be happy as a shopkeeper making things from leather for other people, I would be happy. In fact, I'm happy that you want to marry me."

"I love you," he said.

"I love you, too."

"You know, there's a little store just down the street. It has living quarters in the back, and a small barn out behind the store that is part of the property. It would be perfect for a leather shop and a place for us to live. What do you think?"

"It sounds wonderful."

Ralph stood up and reached out to her. Emma stood up. Ralph wrapped her in his arms and kissed her. It was their first kiss. As soon as their kiss ended. Ralph looked down at her.

"What do you say to going to the bank to talk to them about the shop? The bank owns the building. It is empty right now."

"Okay. I think that is a good idea."

Ralph took Emma's hand and they left the room. It didn't take them long before they were at the bank and talking to the owner of the bank. Since the building had been empty for some time, the banker was glad to have someone who wanted to buy it. Ralph used the money he had saved for the ranch to buy the building.

As soon as the paper work was done, and Ralph and Emma now owned the building, they went to the building to look it over. Once inside the building, they quickly discovered that it was going to take some work to get it just the way they would want it, but for now it needed to be made ready to live in.

"Emma, we can live in the back. but I don't want people to talk about us."

"What do you mean?"

"I will sleep here tonight. You will spend the night at the Kleeman House. We'll get married tomorrow, then you will move in here with me as my wife. I'll spend this afternoon cleaning up the place so we can live here," he said.

"As far as the staying at the Kleeman House tonight, I think that is a good idea if I'm going to be looking for a job as a school teacher, at least until you get your leather business going," she said. "But I will stay and help you clean up the place this afternoon and evening so it is ready for us to live in as soon as we are married."

Ralph smiled at her, then kissed her. They went to work on the living quarters first. They wanted it so it was ready for them to start their married life together. They worked into the evening to get it just right.

Ralph and Emma were married the next day and moved into the building. They didn't have a honeymoon, which was fairly common in those days.

Emma became a school teacher and taught the children of Custer for a good many years. She and Ralph raised five children of their own, three boys and two girls.

Ralph worked hard at their business. It started off slowly because it took him awhile to build up a stock of merchandise to sell. However, it wasn't long and he became very well known in South Dakota, Wyoming, Colorado, and Nebraska, as well as other parts of the country for the quality of his workmanship as a saddle maker as well as other leather items like harnesses for horses.

Emma often thought about how they had met, and how her decision to take a chance and move to a strange land far away from what she knew would turn out. She often said it was the best decision of her life. She was no longer in a strange land, but in a land that she quickly grew to love.

THE CAPTURE OF BEN SULLEY

A fairly tall man in his late twenties was walking down the street of Custer in the Dakota Territory. He had a gun on his hip and a rifle in his hand. He had the appearance of a man who had walked a very long way. His shirt was coated with sweat and his boots were covered with dust and dirt. The look on his face was that of a man who was not only very tired, but also very angry. In fact, he was downright mad.

When he got to the Golden Nugget Saloon, he turned, stepped up on the boardwalk and walked up to the swinging doors and looked inside. He stood there for a moment just looking around the inside of the saloon as if he was looking for someone. The man finally pushed open the swinging doors and went inside.

He walked up to the bar, laid his rifle on the bar and ordered a beer. The barkeeper poured him a beer and set it down in front of the man. The man paid for the beer, then just stood at the bar and looked at it.

"Something wrong with the beer?" the barkeeper asked.

"No," the man said.

The man picked up the beer and took a sip. He then took a long draw of the cool liquid and swallowed it. After taking a deep breath, he turned around and leaned back against the bar. He rested his right hand very close to his pistol while holding the mug of beer in his left hand. It seemed to him that everyone was looking at him. That was all right with the man, because he was looking back at them.

He was really looking for one individual, the one who stole his horse and saddle. He had not seen the man up close who stole his horse, but he had seen him riding away with it. There were men in the saloon who looked similar to the one he had seen, but he wasn't sure if one of them was the man he was looking for.

"My name is Frank Russell," he announced as he looked around the saloon. "I was camping a few miles this side of Hell Canyon when my horse was stolen. That forced me to walk for almost two days just to get here."

"Anyone who steals a man's horse and leaves the man miles from anywhere where he can get food or water should be horsewhipped, and then hung for horse stealing. I want to make it clear. If the man who stole my horse returns him to me, I will spare his life. If I have to take my horse away from that person, I will shoot him dead without a second thought."

Frank noticed that there were a lot of people looking around the room at the others. It was as if they were looking to see which one of the men in the saloon was the one who stole the man's horse. They seemed to want to know if the man who stole the horse was among them.

"I don't think anyone in this saloon would steal a man's horse and leave him on foot miles from anywhere," the barkeeper said. "I know most of the people in here. They're good people."

"You said you know most of the people in here. Who are the people in here that you do not know?" Frank asked.

Frank didn't turn to look at the barkeeper. He continued to look at the people in the saloon. He was looking in the hope of seeing someone who looked nervous. Someone who seemed to be looking for a way out, or a way to escape.

"Well. Let's see. I don't know that old man sitting in the corner."

Frank looked at the old man. It was easy for Frank to see that he was not the one who stole his horse. The man who stole his horse was bigger and not dressed the same. He was also a lot younger.

"Anyone else?"

"The young man sitting behind Flo. I haven't seen him around here before," the barkeeper said.

The man sitting behind the bar girl slowly moved closer to Flo. Flo tried to move away from him, but he took hold of her arm. As he stood up, he pulled Flo to her feet, then held her in front of him. He drew his gun and tried to take a shot at Frank, but Frank didn't draw his gun. Instead, Frank dove to the floor and quickly scrambled around behind the bar.

"Don't anyone try anything or I'll shoot this pretty girl."

The man was holding his gun at the girl's head. He started to move toward the back of the saloon, keeping Flo in front of him. When he got to the backdoor, he pushed it open. He stood in the open door for a minute looking at the men in the saloon.

"Anybody who tries to follow me will not live past this door."

Suddenly, the man pushed Flo toward those in the saloon. Flo stumbled forward and was caught by one of the men sitting at a table in the saloon. The man quickly pushed Flo out of harm's way.

The man who stole Frank's horse slammed the door shut and was gone. No one seemed to be in any hurry to follow the man, and possibly get himself shot.

Frank stood up and moved around in front of the bar. He looked at Flo.

"Are you all right, Miss?" he asked.

"Yes, I think so."

Frank looked around the room. Everyone seemed to be looking at him.

All of a sudden, a man came barging into the saloon. He had a gun in his hand and the badge of a town sheriff on his shirt. He looked around.

"What's been going on here?"

"I came in this saloon looking for the man who stole my horse and saddle. I apparently found him, but he escaped out the backdoor after firing a shot at me."

"Who are you?"

"I'm Frank Russell."

"Frank Russell? The Frank Russell?"

"Well, I'm the only Frank Russell I know of, Sheriff."

"It's my understanding that you are a Pinkerton agent. Is that right?"

"Yes, that's right."

"And some guy got away with your horse?" the sheriff said with a grin.

"Yes, but I fail to see the humor in it. I was returning from a case I just finished in Cheyenne. The trial was held there. I'm on my way to Rapid City where I'm to get a new assignment. I wasn't after anyone, at least until the guy stole my horse. As far as I'm concerned, the guy who stole my horse is my assignment."

"Do you know who it was that stole your horse?" the sheriff asked with a more serious tone in his voice.

"No. I was hoping someone here could tell me the man's name, and hopefully be able to give me some idea of where he might have gone."

The sheriff looked around the saloon. It seemed that everyone was looking at him. They all were wondering what the sheriff was going to do.

"Listen up," the sheriff said while looking around the room. "Do any of you know who the man was that took a shot at Mr. Russell?"

It took a minute or so before the old man slowly raised his hand. It was the old man that the barkeeper had pointed out as one of those he didn't know. He looked scared half to death.

"Do you know who the guy was who shot at Mr. Russell?" the sheriff asked.

"Yes, sir."

"What is his name?" Frank asked.

The old man looked around, then looked at Frank.

"The young man sitting behind Flo. I haven't seen him around here before," the barkeeper said.

The man sitting behind the bar girl slowly moved closer to Flo. Flo tried to move away from him, but he took hold of her arm. As he stood up, he pulled Flo to her feet, then held her in front of him. He drew his gun and tried to take a shot at Frank, but Frank didn't draw his gun. Instead, Frank dove to the floor and quickly scrambled around behind the bar.

"Don't anyone try anything or I'll shoot this pretty girl."

The man was holding his gun at the girl's head. He started to move toward the back of the saloon, keeping Flo in front of him. When he got to the backdoor, he pushed it open. He stood in the open door for a minute looking at the men in the saloon.

"Anybody who tries to follow me will not live past this door."

Suddenly, the man pushed Flo toward those in the saloon. Flo stumbled forward and was caught by one of the men sitting at a table in the saloon. The man quickly pushed Flo out of harm's way.

The man who stole Frank's horse slammed the door shut and was gone. No one seemed to be in any hurry to follow the man, and possibly get himself shot.

Frank stood up and moved around in front of the bar. He looked at Flo.

"Are you all right, Miss?" he asked.

"Yes, I think so."

Frank looked around the room. Everyone seemed to be looking at him.

All of a sudden, a man came barging into the saloon. He had a gun in his hand and the badge of a town sheriff on his shirt. He looked around.

"What's been going on here?"

"I came in this saloon looking for the man who stole my horse and saddle. I apparently found him, but he escaped out the backdoor after firing a shot at me."

"Who are you?"

"I'm Frank Russell."

"Frank Russell? The Frank Russell?"

"Well, I'm the only Frank Russell I know of, Sheriff."

"It's my understanding that you are a Pinkerton agent. Is that right?"

"Yes, that's right."

"And some guy got away with your horse?" the sheriff said with a grin.

"Yes, but I fail to see the humor in it. I was returning from a case I just finished in Cheyenne. The trial was held there. I'm on my way to Rapid City where I'm to get a new assignment. I wasn't after anyone, at least until the guy stole my horse. As far as I'm concerned, the guy who stole my horse is my assignment."

"Do you know who it was that stole your horse?" the sheriff asked with a more serious tone in his voice.

"No. I was hoping someone here could tell me the man's name, and hopefully be able to give me some idea of where he might have gone."

The sheriff looked around the saloon. It seemed that everyone was looking at him. They all were wondering what the sheriff was going to do.

"Listen up," the sheriff said while looking around the room. "Do any of you know who the man was that took a shot at Mr. Russell?"

It took a minute or so before the old man slowly raised his hand. It was the old man that the barkeeper had pointed out as one of those he didn't know. He looked scared half to death.

"Do you know who the guy was who shot at Mr. Russell?" the sheriff asked.

"Yes, sir."

"What is his name?" Frank asked.

The old man looked around, then looked at Frank.

"Well."

"It was Ben Sulley who took the shot at you."

"How is it you know his name?" Frank asked.

"I've known him from when he was a boy. His Ma lives on a ranch not far from here. Her married name is Waters. George Waters is her second husband. Her first husband was Randolph Sulley, Ben's father. He died in prison after he was found guilty of cattle rustlin'. He died in prison some years back. His kid growed up to be almost as mean as his father."

"I've heard of Randolph Sulley," Frank said. "Where do I find Waters' place?"

"It's about five miles back toward Hell Canyon. It's off the road about a mile and half."

"Do you think he would go back there?"

"No. Waters drove the kid off his ranch a couple of years ago. He told him that he would kill him on sight if he ever showed up at his ranch. His ranch hands were told to shoot him on sight, too."

"Can you think of any place else he might go to hide?"

"I'm not sure, but I hear tell that he has a hidin' place somewhere west of Hill City. It's back in the hills somewhere, so I'm told."

"Any idea why he needed my horse?"

"Yeah. He probably ran his horse to death. It wouldn't be the first time he rode a horse to death. He's just plain mean."

"Why would he ride his horse to death?"

"My guess is he had the sheriff from New Castle, Wyoming after him. He was probably headed for Hill City. He knows the area west of Hill City pretty well. It's easy to lose someone in there. From there he could head into the backcountry and return to his hide-out."

"You have any idea where he might have his hide-out?"

"Well, I here tell it's somewhere close to White Tail Peak. He's probably hidin' out in one of them draws up in that area. I can't get ya any closer than that," the old man said.

"Where is White Tail Peak?"

"Oh, it's about four or five miles straight west of that little settlement of Rochford, I think it's called."

"Thanks. Sheriff, you know where I can get a couple of horses?"

"You going after him?"

"You can put money on it."

"You can get a couple of good horses at the livery stable and blacksmith's shop"

"Thanks."

As soon as Frank got a saddle horse and a packhorse, he went to the General Store where he purchased a saddle and supplies. Within a couple of hours, he was ready to start out after the man who had stolen his horse. He went prepared to hunt Ben Sulley down no matter how long it took.

Frank rode toward Hill City. When he got to Hill City, it was late in the day. He decided that it would probably not make any difference if he spent the night there before heading into the backcountry. He took his horses to the blacksmith's shop and stable. He put his horses up there and had the blacksmith take care of them.

He then walked to the hotel and got a room at the hotel for the night. He got cleaned up, a good meal and some much needed rest.

When morning came, Frank went to the Hill City Café and had a good breakfast. He got his horses from the blacksmith, then headed for Rochford.

Frank took his time getting to the little settlement of Rochford. The last thing he wanted was for Ben Sulley to know that there was someone after him.

When he arrived in Rochford, Frank rode up to one of the hitching rails in front of the general store. He stepped out of the saddle, and tied his horses to one of the hitching rails then looked around. He didn't see anyone. However, there were three horses tied to the other hitching rail.

Rochford had only one wood building, and several tents used by prospectors. The building was a combination general store and saloon. The saloon was along one wall. There were only two tables near the bar. The rest of the building was the general store.

Frank drew his rifle from the saddle scabbard. After taking another quick look around and not seeing anyone who might do him harm, he turned and walked into the store. He walked up to the barkeeper and set his rifle down on the bar.

"What can I do for you?" the barkeeper asked.

"I was wondering if you could tell me how to get to White Tail Peak?"

"What in the world would you want to go up there for? Ain't nothin' up there but trees and rocks."

"I hear tell there are some pretty good places to get away from people."

The barkeeper just looked at him. He noticed that Frank carried a pistol hung low on his right leg, and he had set a new model of the Winchester repeating rifle on the bar. The barkeeper got the feeling that this man knew how to use both of the weapons he carried. He also thought that this man might be on the run, but he was not sure if it was from the law.

"It's kinda hard to get there."

"I still want to know how to get there?"

"You take the road west out of town for about three miles. You'll find a narrow trail off on the right side. If you take that trail, it will wind around a bit, but you'll get to White Tail Peak."

"Is there anyone living up there that you know about?"

"There are a couple of cabins just before you get to the trail, but none I know about once you turn off the road onto the narrow trail to the peak."

"Thanks," Frank said.

Frank walked out of the general store. On his way out he noticed that there were three men sitting at a table. One of them had been watching him pretty close while Frank talked to the barkeeper.

Once outside, he walked up to his horses. He looked off toward where White Tail Peak was located. He couldn't see the peak from there, but he could see a lot of forest. There was little doubt in Frank's mind that it would be easy to find several places for someone to ambush him.

He untied his horses and saddled up, then turned his horses away from the hitching rail. Taking his time, he started out of the settlement. It was slow going to get to the trail he was to take to the peak. The road leading to the trail was not much more than a trail itself.

When Frank reached the trail he was to take to the peak, he turned up the trail. He only went about two hundred yards before he stopped. He eased his horses off the trail and into the thick forest. He stepped out of the saddle, then led his horses around behind an outcropping of rocks. Frank tied his horses to a tree.

As soon as his horses were hidden, he moved back toward the road and hunkered down behind a tree that had fallen over several years before. From there, he could see anyone who rode by on the road. He could also see if anyone turned up the trail to follow him.

Frank was a patient man. He waited. He was sure that someone would be coming along the road, and it would probably be the man who watched him leave the store. He was also sure that whoever it was, he would probably be going to where Sulley was located to tell him that there was a man looking for him.

It turned out that Frank didn't have long to wait. One of the men he had seen in the general store was coming along the road. He stopped at the place where the trail left the road. The man stopped and looked at the ground. It was clear to Frank that the man was checking to see if Frank had taken the trail. Frank could see the smile on the man's face. Then the man turned around and headed back to the road.

Frank went back in the woods and got his horses. He got back in the saddle then slowly rode out to the road and began following the man along the road. He was watchful to make sure that the man did not see him. Frank had only gone about a mile when the tracks made by the man turned off on what looked like a deer trail.

Thinking that Sulley may not be too far back in the forest, Frank concealed his horses back in the woods across the road from the deer trail. Going on foot with his rifle in his hand, he followed the tracks left by the man who had turned onto the deer trail. He walked alongside the deer trail so he wouldn't leave any tracks for anyone to see, and stayed back in among the trees so he wouldn't be seen. It was slow going, but with the sun shining it was easy to see that the tracks left by the man showed that he was still on the deer trail.

Frank had been walking along for awhile before he saw a small cabin built in front of a cliff. There was smoke coming out of the chimney. There was a stack of wood cut for a fireplace at the end of the cabin. The front of the cabin had two windows with a door between them. There were no horses tied to the hitching rail in front of the cabin.

Frank wondered where the man who he had followed had put his horse. The only thing he could think of was there had to be a corral or a barn somewhere not too far from the cabin.

Frank began moving around to the front of the cabin, staying back in the woods so he was out of sight. He quickly discovered there was a small barn and corral on the other side of the cabin. There were three horses in the corral. The barn didn't look like it could hold more than three or four horses. It looked like it was more for storing hay and feed for the horses.

Frank immediately recognized one of the horses as his horse. It was the one Sulley had stolen from him.

He started to make plans on how he was going to capture Ben Sulley, and get his horse back. Frank knelt down at the edge of the forest behind a rather large bush and stared at the cabin and its surroundings. At this point, he was just watching to see if anyone came to the cabin or left it while he worked out a plan in his head.

Time went by slowly for Frank, but it was not wasted. He was working over several plans in his head, trying to decide which one might give him the results he wanted, that being capturing Sulley, getting his horse back, then getting out of there in one piece. He smiled to himself as he decided on one of his plans. It wasn't foolproof, it might not even have been his best plan, but if it worked, he would get the results he was looking for, and still be able to get out in one piece.

Frank began looking around for something that might help him with his plan. That was when he saw a ladder leaning up against the cabin next to the wood pile. The end of the ladder was almost leaning against the chimney.

He quickly moved around in the forest so he was at the end of the cabin where there were no windows, but where the pile of cut wood had been stacked. Frank moved carefully to the end of the cabin. He looked up at the roof and the top of the chimney. He smiled to himself. Frank picked out three short pieces of wood that would work for what he planned to do.

Being as careful as he could not to make a sound, he climbed up to the roof next to the chimney. He placed the three pieces of wood over the top of the chimney to block off the smoke.

He knelt down while he waited for the cabin to fill up with smoke. He checked his guns and prepared himself for what would happen next. Frank was counting on the smoke forcing the men inside to come out.

Suddenly, the cabin door flew open and three men came running out of the smoke-filled cabin. They were coughing and stumbling around as they came out of the cabin. The smoke had made it hard for them to breath as well as hard to see.

"Drop your guns, and lay down on the ground," Frank called out as he held his rifle on the three outlaws.

One of the men drew his gun and fired a couple of shots toward the corner of the cabin. He couldn't see Frank because of the smoke in his eyes. Frank was not at the corner of the cabin. He was still on the roof. Frank fired one shot and instantly killed the man.

"Drop your guns and lay face down on the ground, NOW!"

The two remaining men dropped their guns and laid down on the ground. Since the outlaws couldn't see Frank, he was able to get down off the roof quickly.

Frank walked up to the outlaws and picked up their guns. He leaned his rifle up against the porch of the cabin, then drew his pistol. With his pistol in his hand, and while watching the men, he moved over to the small corral and took a rope off the only horse in the corral that had a saddle still on it.

He returned to the two outlaws and tied them up. He tied their hands behind their backs, stood them up, then put the end of the rope over a limb of a tree and pulled it up tight. It caused the two to bend over at the waist. That position severely limited their ability to move. It was a very uncomfortable position to be in.

With the outlaws restrained, Frank went and got the horses from the corral, and the two horses he had left in the woods. He saddled up the outlaws' horses and his own horse then led them over to the two outlaws.

Taking the outlaws one at a time, he put them on the horses and tied them to the saddles in such a way that if they tried to escape, they would end up hanging themselves. He then tied the horses together.

Once he was ready, he mounted up and began the trek back to Custer. It took two days to get to Custer. By the time the two outlaws arrived, they were more than willing to get out of the saddle and into a jail cell. They were also glad to have the ropes around their necks taken off them.

Frank returned the horses he had gotten from the blacksmith's stable. It was time to wait for the judge to come to Custer to hold the trial.

While they waited for the judge, Frank and the sheriff took turns guarding the prisoners. It was only four days before the judge arrived and held court.

Ben Sulley was tried for the murder of a bank teller, robbery, and horse stealing. The other outlaw as tried for murdering a bank teller and robbery. Both outlaws were found guilty of the charges against them, and sentenced to hang.

After the trial, Frank Russell saddled his horse and went on to Rapid City where he got his next assignment.

ZACKERY JOHNSON, GOVERNMENT AGENT

Government agent, Zackery Johnson was riding across the prairie on his way to one of the reservations when he thought he saw what looked like a camp in the distance. The camp was in among some cottonwood trees along the bank of a creek. He stopped and reached behind for his field glasses. He took his field glasses out of his saddle bags and put them up to his eyes and looked at the camp. He could see a small covered wagon under a large cottonwood tree. He did not see any horses or mules that would be needed to pull the wagon, but they could have been on the other side of the wagon.

He was surprised to see what looked like five people lying on the ground in a neat row next to the wagon. He could not tell from the distance who the people were or what they were doing there. It didn't make sense to Zackery that anyone would take a nap at this time of day. It was just shortly after noon.

Not sure what was going on there, he began to scan the area around the camp very carefully. Several hundred yards off to the south of the wagon, on the same side of the creek as the wagon, he could see what looked like a good number of buffalo, maybe fifty or sixty of them. Most of the buffalo were lying on the ground while a few were grazing. He quickly realized that the buffalo were simply resting and showed no real interest in what was close by them. One of the buffalo rolled over on the ground, and another stood up and shook the dust off after wallowing in the dirt of a shallow buffalo wallow. The buffalo didn't seem to know about the wagon or the people that were only a short distance away from them.

After looking around in all directions, Zackery decided to ride down to the creek and find out what was going on. After putting his field glasses back in his saddlebags, he started toward the wagon.

Knowing that buffalo can be unpredictable, he stayed in a position where the wagon would be between him and the buffalo. He was sure that there was something wrong. It was early afternoon. No one would be napping so close to resting buffalo unless something was wrong, or they didn't know the buffalo were there.

The closer Zackery got to the wagon, the more he began to realize that it was not some people simply taking a nap. It was the bodies of five people he had seen from the ridge. As he got even closer, he could see that there was a woman, two adult men and two teenage boys, and that they had been dead for several days.

Zackery rode up to the wagon and looked around before he stepped out of the saddle and tied his horse to the wagon. He studied the ground around the wagon. It wasn't long before he figured out what must have happened there.

All the signs indicated that the family had been attacked by a small group of men, maybe four or five. The two men, and the two teenagers had been shot, then scalped. The woman looked like she had just been shot.

Based on the tracks that led away from the area of the wagon, there had to have been at least one other woman and at least three, possibly four children walking, and four men on horses. The tracks also showed that the horses were shod. That led him to believe that this may have been done by white men.

Zackery slowly began putting together in his mind what had probably happened. Four, maybe five, white men had come upon the wagon and the people who had stopped for the night to rest after a hard day of traveling. Seeing white men approaching, the people with the wagon probably didn't expect any danger and simply greeted them.

The white men suddenly attacked the people, shooting the men and teenage boys before they could defend themselves. The one woman shot might have tried to get way, or she tried to fight back. After killing those who had greeted them, they took the remaining members of the party as prisoners with the idea of selling them to the Indians.

Since it appeared as if the travelers who were killed had been dead for a day or two, it appeared to Zackery that the buffalo probably came into the area after the fight, and were just resting after a morning of grazing on the prairie grasses and drinking from the creek. The fact that there were no buffalo tracks anywhere near the wagon supported that idea.

It crossed Zackery's mind that the white men killed the small party of people thinking that they were buffalo hunters. However, that didn't seem logical. Very few buffalo hunters had women and children with them. If there had been a fight between the raiders and the people while the buffalo were there, the buffalo would not still be there. They would have left the area.

Zackery looked off in the direction the tracks indicated that the people had gone. He knew that there were several small groups of Indians in the area. He knew several of the chiefs. Of the ones he knew about, they would not attack a small group of white people without cause. The Indians would not have laid out the bodies in a neat row. That thought was enough to make him think that they had been attacked by white men.

When he figured that he had all the evidence available, the shod horses, cowboy boots, the way the victims were shot and laid out, he was sure it was white men who had done it. The reason was unknown. Was it planned or was it a spur of the moment decision to take the survivors prisoners and sell them to one of the northern tribes? He had no answers, but he knew he had to try to save the survivors.

Zackery began going through everything he could find in the wagon in an effort to figure out who the travelers were. It didn't take him long to find out the last name of at least some of the victims. He found a Bible under the seat of the wagon that had the family name written in it. The family name was Johansson.

The first order of business was to bury the dead. Once that was done, it was time to find those who had killed them. But since it was getting late by the time he had buried all the victims, he decided that it soon would be too dark to follow the tracks left by the raiders and their victims.

Zackery set up camp near a couple of trees along the creek. After fixing his dinner, he let his fire burn out, then fell asleep on his bedroll.

Zackery slept late after working so hard to bury the victims. When he woke, the sun was already up. He sat up and looked around. Behind him he saw six young braves sitting on Indian ponies just looking at him.

Zackery slowly stood up and turned to face them. It wasn't until he had a chance to look at them that he recognized one of the braves. It was the son of one of the chiefs he had befriended some years ago.

"Swift Eagle, it is good to see you again."

"It is good to see you, too, my friend. What brings you so far from home."

"I was on my way to the white man's village called Rapid City. I came upon this wagon and several dead men and a dead woman. I buried them yesterday."

"We saw the buffalo early this morning and came down from the hill," Swift Eagle said as he pointed to the hill. "We also saw the wagon and came here to see why it was here."

"Do you know anything about the people who had been here?"

"No."

"The people I buried had been murdered. There were at least several children and one woman who were taken away."

"Do you think Indians did this?"

"No. I think white men did it. Have you seen any white men with a woman and children walking? There would have been four mules with them, and at least four men on horseback."

"I did see such men on horses? The woman and four children were walking. They were leading four mules. Woman and four children were tied together. Rope held by a big man."

"Have you ever seen these men before?"

"Yes. I have seen the big man. He is no good. He very mean man."

"Do you know where he might be going?"

"Not sure. I think he was going up north to sell the woman and children to Indians. You go after them?"

"Yes."

"If you hurry, you might catch them before they sell them to Indians up north."

"Thanks. I best get started."

"Take care my friend," Swift Eagle said.

"I will. You take care, and tell your father that I wish him well."

"I will."

Zackery watched as Swift Eagle nodded his head, then turned his horse and rode off to the east with the five braves following behind him.

Zackery packed up his belongs and saddled his horse. It was good that his horse had been able to get some rest. It would be a hard ride to catch up with the men he was after.

As soon as Zackery was ready, he mounted up and headed north. He set a gait that was easy on the horse, but covered a lot of ground. He knew they had a good head start on him, but he had to catch up with them before they sold their prisoners, or he might never get them back.

Zackery rode from sunup to sundown. He would give his horse a break every so often by getting off and walking his horse. Whenever they came to a creek or stream, he would give his horse a chance to drink and eat a little of the lush grass that grew along the bank.

It was three days of hard riding before he saw fresh signs of the men he was after. He knew he was getting close.

Off to the west was a rise in the prairie floor. He thought it might give him a chance to see ahead, maybe even see the men he was after.

He rode up onto the rise, stepped out of the saddle and took his field glasses from his saddlebags. He could make out several individuals. It was clear that there were several people riding horses and some walking.

Zackery scanned the area looking for a place where he might be able to get a better look at who was in front of him. He noticed a hill they were just passing. He was sure he could swing around the backside of the hill and get closer to them. If he could get closer without being seen, he might be able to figure out a way to rescue the prisoners.

There was no doubt that it would be hard to rescue the prisoners since there was four men on horses. It would be difficult to deal with the four men while still protecting the prisoners from harm. There was little doubt that he would have to bide his time and wait until an opportunity presented itself.

Zackery followed the band of people as they slowly walked along. It wasn't until they stopped by a creek to set up camp for the night that he thought he might get his chance to rescue the prisoners.

He stopped near the top of a hill that overlooked their camp. Zackery tied his horse to a little scrub pine back off the top of the hill where it could not be seen. He then took his field glasses and crawled up to the top of the hill. He laid down in the grass to watch those at the camp.

While he waited for darkness to cover the land, he watched what was going on. It was clear that the woman and two young girls were put to work fixing dinner for all of them. Two of the men were watching them closely. The two young boys were gathering wood for the fire under the close supervision of one of the men. The big man seemed to be the leader and was watching over everyone. He would often look around in an effort to make sure they were safe.

Zackery took that time to plan what he would do to get the prisoners away from the men keeping them captive, and capture those who had taken them prisoners. He couldn't help but think that his first priority was to get the prisoners away safely.

Time passed slowly as he watched. Just before dark, he saw them tie the woman and the children to trees. He also saw the big man and two of the other men had spread out bedrolls and were lying down on them. The fourth man looked like he was standing guard.

Zackery could see the one standing guard walk around behind the prisoners and check the ropes to make sure they were secure. He then walked over to the fire and poured himself a cup of coffee. The guard took his cup of coffee and moved over to a tree out of the light of the fire. He sat down and leaned back against the tree. The glow of the fire was just enough so that Zackery could see him.

As Zackery watched what was going on, he decided that the first thing he had to do was take out the one standing guard as quickly and quietly as possible. He also needed to do something that would cause a great deal of confusion in the camp.

Timing was important. Zackery gathered up several rounds of ammunition and wrapped them in a piece of cloth. He tucked the piece of cloth in his belt so he could remove it quickly. He then checked his pistols and rifle to make sure they were ready for use. He was ready. It was time to sneak down to the camp at the creek.

Zackery started to move down off the hill. Instead of approaching the camp directly, he went around the camp toward the creek. He moved slowly so he wouldn't make a sound.

Once he was near the creek, he worked his way to where the prisoners were tied. It took him a couple of minutes to get around behind the woman. He looked around and noticed that the children had fallen asleep. He could certainly understand that, as they had been walking for several days.

Zackery slipped up behind the woman. He reached out and put his hand over her mouth. It startled the woman, but he kept her from making any noise.

"Don't move," Zackery whispered. "I'm going to cut you lose, but don't move."

He cut the rope holding her against the tree. She didn't move.

"As soon as you hear the noise, take this knife and cut the children lose and run for the bushes along the creek and get down. Do you understand?"

She nodded. Zackery slowly took his hand off the woman's mouth. He reached around her and laid a knife in her lap. He also reached around her and laid a gun in her lap.

"Use it if you have to, but try not to shoot me."

She turned her head and looked at him. She nodded again.

Zackery then slipped back away from her. He turned and moved over toward the man who was standing guard. Zackery slipped up behind the tree the guard was leaning against.

Being as quiet as he could, he reached around the tree put one hand over the man's mouth as he hit him with the butt of his pistol that he held in his other hand. There was only a slight grunt when the butt of Zackery's gun knocked the guard out cold.

Zackery quickly moved up to the fire and dropped the cloth with the ammunition in it into the fire. He then drew back into the darkness behind a large cottonwood tree, and waited.

It was only a couple of minutes before all hell broke loose. The ammunition began to explode, scattering ash, small sticks, sparks, hot coals, and flames from the fire. Some of it hitting the men who had been sleeping.

The three men who had been sleeping were certainly wide awake now, but they were confused by the 'shots' fired. The hot coals and burning sticks flying through the air didn't help.

"Drop the guns and put your hands up."

The three looked around, but they couldn't see anyone. Zackery stayed behind a large cottonwood tree. One of the men grabbed for a gun and fired a shot in the general direction of the tree, but was cut down quickly by a single shot from Zackery's rifle. The two remaining men raised their hands in the air as they sat on their bedrolls.

"Take off your boots, then stand up and drop your holsters on the ground. One wrong move and you will be shot," Zackery said sharply.

The two men complied with his order. Once they had done what Zackery told them, he stood up and walked over to them.

"Keep an eye on them." Zackery said.

No one answered. The two men were not sure if Zackery was alone, or if there was someone else with him, but they soon found out that he was not alone. One of them turned as if he might want to dive out of sight, but stopped quickly when a shot rang out and the bullet hit right next to his foot.

"The next shot will be the last thing you hear," Zackery said.

Zackery went over to the saddles belonging to the two men. He took the ropes off the saddles. He made a loop in one of the ropes, tossed it over the big man's head and pulled it up tight.

The big man instantly grabbed the rope in an effort to keep it from strangling him. Zackery tossed the other end over the branch of a big cottonwood tree and drew it up until the big man could just barely stand with his feet flat on the ground. Zackery tied the rope off, leaving the big man there.

He went to the other man and did the same thing to him. After both men had ropes around their necks, Zackery tied their hands behind them. Once he had the two men tied so they could not do anything, he walked over to the one he had knocked out. He was still out, so he simply hogtied him and left him lying on the ground.

Zackery walked over to the woman. She had the children gathered closely around her. He was not sure if she was comforting the children, or they were comforting her. She looked up at him.

"Ma'am, you are safe now. What is your name?"

"Martha Johansson. What is your name?"

"Zackery Johnson. I'm a government Agent. Are all these children yours?

"No. The two girls are mine. I am the aunt of the two boys."

"The sun will be up soon. I think it would be a good idea if you fix the children breakfast."

"What are we going to do now?"

"Well, ma'am, I think I will take the mules and go back and get your wagon and bring it back here so you don't have to walk any further. This is a good place for you to spend a couple of days to rest. You will have enough food and water here."

"What about these men? What are you going to do with them?"

"I think I will tie them to the trees so you can feed and water them. Once I get back, I'll take them to the nearest county seat for trial.

"Now, don't spend any time with them. Feed and water them like you would any animal but make sure you don't let them loose. Keep that gun handy, but don't let them get their hands on it. Keep the children away from them. You think you can do that?"

"Yes, but wouldn't it be easier if we all went together to get the wagon?"

Zackery looked at the children, then at the men tied to the tree. He thought about it. If the children rode double and the men were on the mules, it could work.

"I think we could do that."

Zackery and the children gathered wood for a fire. After the fire was going good, Martha and the two girls fixed breakfast. After Zackery finished eating, he fed the prisoners.

Once everything was cleaned up, and the fire had been put out, Zackery buried the man he shot, then tied the prisoners on the backs of the mules. There were enough horses for everyone else to have one to ride, except for the smallest girl. She rode with Zackery.

The prisoners didn't give anyone any trouble. It had been made clear that if they gave anyone any trouble, any trouble at all, he would be buried out on the prairie.

When they got back to where the wagon had been left, Zackery spent a day with what was left of the Johansson party. He helped them get organized and on their way.

As soon as they were on their way, Zackery took his prisoners to the nearest county seat. He held them in jail until the circuit judge could come. A trial was held and the three men were found guilty of several murders and sentenced to be hung by the neck until dead.

After the sentences had been carried out, Zackery went on to Rapid City to report what he had been doing. He then got his next assignment.

LIFE AFTER THE WAR

After the Civil War. Sergeant Fred Wells returned to his farm and an empty house. His first born and his wife had died during childbirth while he was fighting at Gettysburg on July 3, 1863 under the command of General Longstreet.

With the war over, he felt as if there was nothing left for him in northern Kentucky. He decided to sell the farm and leave Kentucky. It held just too many bad memories for him to stay on the small farm.

Fred's neighbor had shown an interest in the farm. He sold the farm to his neighbor, then packed up what few things he had left that he wanted to keep. Fred put them in his small covered wagon. He harnessed his team of horses and tied his saddle horse to the back of the wagon. Fred was almost ready to leave, but he had one more thing to do. He walked out to the graves of his wife and child to say goodbye.

After visiting the graves of his wife and child, Fred took one last look at the home he and his family had shared, then got in his wagon and headed west for the Dakota Territory. It was his hope that he would find a place where he could settle down in peace. A place where he could forget about his past, or at the very least, put it behind him.

Fred figured that moving to the Dakota Territory would be the best thing for him. No one would know him, and he could start a new life. Little did he know what the future held for him.

Fred Wells had been traveling for almost three months. It was a bright sunny day as Fred sat on his wagon with his saddle horse tied behind. The road he was traveling was a long, narrow and dusty road that wound its way across the prairie of the Dakota Territory. He was enjoying the cool breeze and the peace and soft rhythmic sound as his horses plodded along.

Suddenly, his peace and quiet from traveling alone was disturbed when he was set upon by a small band of Indians. His experience in the Army had taught him it was often better to stand and fight, than to fight while running, especially if it was just a few attackers.

Instead of trying run from the Indians, Fred reined up his team of horses then jumped in the back of his wagon. He grabbed his Henry repeating rifle and waited for the Indians to get closer.

When the Indians began firing at him, he returned fire. He dropped three of the Indians very quickly. The remaining four quickly turned and rode away from him until they were out of range of his rifle. Everything was quiet again.

The Indians seemed to be confused. It was almost as if they expected him to try to run from them. They were confused by his stopping and taking them on in a face-to-face fight.

Fred remained in the back of his wagon while he watched the Indians in order to see what they were going to do. To his surprise, they simply sat on their horses and watched him. They made no move to attack him again or go to the aid of their friends.

After waiting for what seemed like an eternity, but it was only about fifteen minutes, Fred thought about moving on. He had no idea what they might do if he started to move. He decided to wait a few more minutes.

When the Indians didn't make a move, or advance toward him, he decided he would move back to the seat of the wagon and try to leave. With his pistol in his holster and his Henry repeating rifle on the seat in easy reach, he moved back to the seat, picked up the reins and started to move the wagon forward.

He kept a close eye on the Indians to see what they were going to do. He soon discovered that they just sat on their horses and watched him leave.

For the next hour or so, Fred made it a point to keep an eye out to see if they were going to attack him again. The last thing he saw before going over a low ridge was the Indians going to where those he had shot were lying. He was relieved to see they were not coming after him.

Just to be sure that they had not chosen to follow him in the hope of finding another opportunity to kill him and get his horses, Fred continued on into the dark of night. The only light he had was from a clear sky and an almost full moon.

It was well into the night when he came upon a creek. Fred carefully drove his team of horses across the creek, then turned and moved down stream to a grove of cottonwood trees. He set up his camp there, but did not build a fire. He knew that a fire at night could be seen for miles out on the open prairie. He had heard that Indians would not fight at night. If he remembered it correctly, he was told it was because their spirts would wonder forever, and they would never get to the happy hunting ground. He wasn't sure he believed that about the Indians, but there was no sense in taking any chances.

Just to be on the safe side, rather than sleep in the wagon as he had often done, he laid out his bedroll about fifteen feet from his wagon next to an old cottonwood tree that had fallen over many years ago. He was far enough away from his wagon to be safe, but close enough to hear anyone who might come close to it. He tied his horses to the side of the wagon closest to him. They would certainly let him know if anyone came around.

As soon as he was ready, he leaned his rifle up against the fallen tree only inches from his bedroll, then laid down to rest. It wasn't long and he was asleep.

When the sun was just getting ready to come up over the horizon, he woke. He got up and looked around. He was careful to make sure there was no one close by.

Seeing no one, Fred built a small fire and cooked his breakfast. As soon as he finished eating and put out his fire, he took his horses to the creek for a drink. He noticed that they had eaten all the grass around the wagon where he had left them last night, so he gave them time to eat the grass along the bank of the creek, and get a drink of water while he kept an eye out for any danger that might come his way.

As soon as the horses were ready to travel again, he harnessed his team of horses then hitched them to the wagon. He tied his saddle horse on the rear of the wagon, then continued on his way.

Fred didn't see any more Indians for several days. When he was getting close to the foothills of the Black Hills, he did see a few Indians that were a long way away from him. He was sure they saw him, but didn't seem to pay any attention to him. They rode away from him.

On a late afternoon, some weeks after he was attacked on the prairie, he came to a small ranching community at the southern end of the Black Hills, along the Cheyenne River. The sign at the edge of the settlement read "Edgemont".

Fred drove his wagon down the dusty street to the General Store, the largest building in the settlement. He stepped down from the wagon, then tied his horses to the hitching rail in front of the store. He took a couple of minutes to look around.

It wasn't much of a town, but it was just what he needed. There was a bank, a saloon, a Blacksmith's shop with a stable, and of course, the general store. He couldn't help but think that it was like a lot of the small towns on the prairie he had passed through. However, this one was far enough from what he had left behind that he thought he would feel comfortable living there. But what was more important to him was no one would know him here, or his past.

Since the general store was the largest building on the street, he was sure it was where he could find out almost anything he wanted to know about the town, and what was going on in the surrounding area. He stepped up on the boardwalk, took a quick look around again, then opened the door and walked into the store.

He first noticed two women standing behind the counter. They looked to be very close in age, and they looked very much alike. As he walked up to the counter, the women turned and looked at him. One of them smiled. He found her smile very pleasant.

"May I help you?" she asked.

"Ah, yes, ma'am. I'm looking for a place to settle down."

"Welcome. You've come to the right place. I'm Marcie, and this is my older sister Martha."

"Nice to meet you," he said staring at Marcie.

"You said you were looking for a place to settle. Do you know what you want to do?"

"Oh, ah, yes. Yes, I do. I have farmed in the past. I was thinking that I might like to farm again, and maybe raise a few cattle."

"Like I said, you have come to the right place. There is land here to do both."

"Who would I have to talk to about obtaining some land?"

"That would be me," came a male voice from behind him.

Fred turned to see who was behind him. His jaw fell open when he saw the man.

"I'll be darned. If it isn't Sergeant Wells," the man said.

"Captain Palmer!"

"In the flesh, or what there is left of it."

Fred looked at him. At first, he hadn't noticed that the captain was leaning on a crutch.

"I don't use the 'captain' any more. It's just Bill, or Mr. Palmer. I think you can call me, Bill."

"I don't use the 'sergeant' any more either. It's Fredrick or Fred. I wondered what happened to you after Gettysburg. I saw you fall. I was told later that you died."

"Well, as you can see, I'm very much alive. This is my wife. Martha."

"It is nice to meet you, Mrs. Palmer."

"Oh, in case you have not been properly introduced, this is Marcie. She is Martha's sister. So, you want to farm or ranch around here?" Palmer asked.

"I thought the land around here would make good ground for either," Fred said.

"It does do that. Why don't you come to dinner tonight? I have a map of the area. After dinner, I'll show you where there is some land to be settled in this area. In the morning we can go and look it over if you see something that interests you."

"It won't be too much trouble, will it?"

"No, no trouble at all," Martha said with a smile. "You are more than welcome."

"I'll find a place to put my wagon, then ride out to your place."

"Why don't you bring your wagon on out to our place. There's a big beautiful tree next to the corral. You can put your wagon there and your animals in the corral. There's a pump for water close by, too," Marcie said.

"That's a good idea," Bill said.

"Okay," Fred said. "All I need to know is where is your place located."

"We are not busy right now. I could show you the way," Marcie said.

Fred looked around to see if it was all right with Bill and Martha. He saw Martha smiling.

"It's fine," Bill said. "Marcie is done here. She can ride out with you and show you where to set up camp. We'll be along soon."

"Thank you," Fred said.

Marcie walked around the counter and started out the door. Fred followed her to his wagon. He had helped her up on the wagon just as a young man came riding into town. The young man rode up to the wagon just as Fred sat down on the seat. He looked up at Fred, then at Marcie.

"Where do you think you're going?" the young man said sharply.

"That's none of your business," Marcie replied sharply.

"Get down off that wagon, right now."

"You have no right to talk to me like that. I'm not your wife, and I'm certainly not even your girlfriend.

"I said get down off that wagon," he said as he reached up and grabbed her by the arm.

"Let go of me."

"Hold on there. You take your hands off her," Fred said, his voice quiet yet forceful.

"Who the hell are you anyway. You don't belong around here."

"He is a friend of mine, that's who he is," Marcie said sharply.

"We'll see about that. You're my girl and that ends it."

"I told you a long time ago, Tim Smith, that I wouldn't be seen with you, and I certainly wouldn't marry you if you were the last man on earth."

"I think it would be a good idea if you would just go about your business and leave this woman alone," Fred said.

"Who do you think you are telling me what to do?"

"I'm somebody you don't want to make mad. I suggest you move on before I get mad. I also suggest you leave Miss Marcie alone, and stop bothering her."

Tim looked right at Fred. Who is this guy, was the question running through his head. No one had ever talked to him like that before.

All of a sudden, Bill Palmer showed up. He had a shotgun in one hand and his crutch in the other as he came around from the back of the wagon. Leaning on the crutch, he swung the shotgun up so it was pointed at Tim.

"Tim, I told you that if you bother my sister-in-law, I would blow your head off. Now get out of here before I do it right now."

Fred could see the fear on Tim's face. That shotgun could really backup a man's statement and put a period on the end of a sentence.

"This isn't the end of this."

"It darn well better be, or you won't live to see your next birthday. I'm going to talk to your father, and let him know that his son's life expectancy is very short if he doesn't keep you away from her. You got that?" Bill said.

Fred could see Tim was shaking. He had seen that kind of fear on faces of many men going into battlefield many times.

"I got it. I'm going," Tim said.

Bill and Fred watched him as he swung his horse hard around and rode off down the street and on out of town. He never once looked back.

"Do you think that will be the end of it?" Fred asked.

"I doubt it," Bill said. "He's the type that has to push it to the limit. One of these days he is going to push someone too hard and they're going to kill him."

"I think you're right. He's the type who would be more than willing to shoot someone in the back. I'll have to keep my eyes open," Fred said.

"You do that. In the meantime, Marcie, show Fred where he can set up his camp at our place.

Fred nodded then looked at Marcie. He smiled.

"Point the way," Fred said.

Marcie looked at him for a moment, then pointed down the street.

"It's just a little way out of town. Bill has a small ranch. He raises a few horses and trains them."

"He is good at it," Fred said. "He handled a lot of the training of horses for the cavalry for the Army."

"I never knew what he did in the Army. All I know is he was injured during the war. From what was said in the store, I take it you were in the war, too."

"I was, but like Bill, I prefer not to talk about it."

"I will respect your wishes and not ask you about it. Maybe someday you will tell me about it."

"Maybe, and thank you."

"I'm sorry that you had to see Tim like that. He is jealous of anyone who talks to me. It has been that way for years."

"Does he have reason to be jealous?"

"No. I have never stepped out with him, or even hardly talked to him. I make it a point not to talk to him. He thinks he owns anything or anybody he wants just because his father owns the biggest ranch in the area.

"Bill wasn't kidding when he said he was about to shoot him. I think the only reason he doesn't kill him is because he has seen enough killing."

"I'm sure you are right. I certainly can understand how Bill feels about killing. Both of us have seen enough during the war to last a lifetime."

Nothing more was said about it. It wasn't a long ride out to the ranch. Once they arrived, Marcie directed Fred to a place under a large cottonwood tree. He stopped his wagon under the tree, then got down from the wagon. He helped Marcie down.

"What can I do to help?" she asked.

"You can take my saddle horse over to the corral. I'll take care of him as soon as I unhitch the wagon, and get the horses in the corral."

Fred unhitched the horses from the wagon, then took the harness off them and put it in the wagon. He led them over to the corral where he turned them loose.

He looked around for his saddle horse but didn't see it. He went inside the barn and found Marcie brushing his horse. She seemed to be talking to him.

"I hope you're not trying to talk him into running away with you?" Fred said with a smile.

"No. I would never do that. I was just getting to know him. He's a beautiful horse."

"That he is. He's also smart. He knows a pretty girl when he sees one."

Fred could see that his comment made Marcie blush. There was a long moment of silence before either of them said a word. Marcie was the first one to speak.

"You traveled all the way out here by yourself?"

"Yes."

"Wasn't that rather dangerous?"

"I didn't have much trouble. A few Indians attacked me in an effort to get my horses. After we had a little skirmish, they decided they didn't want them after all."

Marcie smiled at him, then turned back to brushing the horse. The more she talked to Fred the more interested in him she became. He was a handsome man, and he was nice. He even seemed at ease when talking to her. She liked that in a man. She turned to say something to him, but all she got was a glimpse of him as he walked out of the barn.

It was only a couple of minutes before he returned to the barn. He was leading his team of horses. He put them in stalls, took a rag and started rubbing down one of the horses.

Nothing much was said between them while he rubbed down his horses, and she brushed his saddle horse. They both seemed to be comfortable just being together, even if they were working and not talking.

It wasn't long before Marcie had finished brushing Fred's horse. She walked over to the stall where Fred was rubbing down the last of his horses. She leaned against the stall and watched Fred. He turned and looked at her.

"You done with my horse?"

"Yes. He's really a nice horse."

"Yes, he is. Maybe you would like to take a ride on him sometime. He is easy to ride."

"I would like that." Marcie said. "I should get inside and get dinner started. Bill and Martha will be home soon."

Fred nodded, then watched her as she walked out of the barn toward the house. She had just stepped in the house out of sight when Fred heard footsteps behind him. He turned around to find Tim Smith standing behind him. He had his gun in his hand.

"Didn't expect to see me so soon, did you?" Tim said.

"As a matter of fact, I didn't, but I should have. You're the kind who has to sneak up on people. You can't meet a man face to face. You're also the kind who doesn't care whose property he trespasses on."

It was Fred's habit to notice everything around him. He noticed that Tim was standing right behind the stall his saddle horse was in.

"You shoot me now and you will die at the end of a rope. I don't have a gun on me, but then you didn't come here to draw against me, did you?"

"No. I came here to beat you within an inch of your life."

"With a gun in your hand?"

"I don't need a gun to beat you within an inch of your life."

"Let me guess. You are going to beat me up to get me to leave so Marcie will be your girl? Right?"

"Something like that."

"You are dumber than I thought. By beating up men, you think it will make Marcie like you. All you will do is make people mad, and they will end up hating you. In fact, you are making me mad just holding that gun on me."

"Yeah, but there's nothing you can do about it."

"I wouldn't take any bets on that. KICK!" Fred yelled.

Before Tim could react, Fred's horse kicked Tim, knocking him across the barn. Tim ended up in a heap on the floor of the barn. The horse had kicked Tim so hard, it broke his right arm in two places as well as a couple of ribs. Tim laid in pain on the floor of the barn.

Fred walked over and picked up Tim's gun. He then walked up to Tim and looked down at him. He pointed Tim's gun right at his face.

"I can't think of one good reason why I shouldn't kill you right here. The next time I see you, I will shoot you on sight. Do you understand that?"

Tim was breathing hard and was in a good deal of pain. He looked up at Fred, and all he could see was the end of his own gun pointed right at him.

"You are in no condition to be riding a horse. I'll get Bill's buckboard and take you home. Just because I take you home so your father can take care of you, doesn't mean that I won't shoot you on sight."

Tim didn't say anything. He just watched as Fred went up to the house. It wasn't long before he returned with Marcie. He harnessed a horse to the buckboard.

As soon as it was ready, Marcie and Fred helped Tim onto the buckboard. Marcie put a blanket over Tim.

Tim looked at her. Marcie looked at him.

"I never want to see you again. Do you understand?" Marcie.

Tim just looked at her for a minute, then nodded that he understood.

"I won't bother you anymore. I promise," he said weakly.

Fred looked at Marcie for a minute, smiled, then drove away. It took Fred a good hour to get to the Smith Ranch.

When he pulled up in front of the ranch house. Mr. Smith stepped outside. He first looked at Fred, but didn't say anything. It wasn't until he saw his son in the back of the buckboard that he spoke.

"What happened?" he said as he moved up alongside the buckboard. "Did you do this to him?"

"No. He did it to himself."

Mr. Smith looked at his son, then at Fred. He was confused by what Fred said.

"I think it would be best if you let him explain. Oh, there is one other thing. You might not want your son playing with guns," Fred said as he handed Tim's gun to Mr. Smith.

Fred waited while Mr. Smith got a couple of ranch hands to help Tim out of the buckboard and into the house. As soon as Tim was out of the buckboard, Fred turned the horse and headed back to Bill Palmer's home.

When he arrived back at the Palmer Ranch, he was met by Marcie, Martha and Bill. By the look on their faces, Fred could see they wanted to know how things went at the Smith Ranch.

"How did it go with Mr. Smith?" Bill asked.

"I think Mr. Smith is not too happy with me. There could be some problems with him, depending on what Tim tells his father."

"Marcie tells me you beat him up pretty bad when he caught you alone in the barn. Is that right?"

"Not entirely. Actually, I never touched him. He just made the mistake of standing behind my horse."

Both Marcie and Bill looked confused by his comment. He thought he should clear things up for them.

"I trained my horse to kick on command. When Tim walked up behind my horse, I just said 'kick'. My horse did, and Tim found himself lying in a heap on the other side of the barn."

Bill and Marcie had a good laugh, then went in the house for dinner. But it was not destined to be a peaceful dinner. They had just about finished when they heard several horses ride into the yard in front of the house. Bill went to the window and looked out. Out in front of the house was Mr. Smith and several of his ranch hands.

"Palmer! You send your guest out here right now, or I'll set your house on fire."

"That sounds like Smith," Fred said.

"It is," Bill replied.

"I'll go out and meet him. This is not your problem," Fred said.

"I'm coming out," Fred called out to Smith. "No need to bring this down on the Palmers."

"Marcie, grab up that shotgun. Go out the back and up to the front corner of the house. Martha, get a rifle and go to the parlor. Put old man Smith in your sights. I want him to know he will be the first to fall," Palmer said. "I'll back up Fred when he goes out."

"Palmer! You've got just five minutes to send your friend out."

Fred moved up beside a window then looked out. There were six men sitting on horses, all of them with rifles in their hands.

"I'm coming out. If any of your men even look like they might try to shoot me, you, Mr. Smith, will be the first to die," Fred said.

Fred looked a Bill. Bill nodded. Fred opened the front door and stepped out on the porch with Bill behind. As soon as they were out on the porch, Bill stepped to Fred's right. Bill had a shotgun pointed right at Smith.

"Before you do something stupid, I must warn you, there are two shotguns and a rifle pointed at you and your men. The rifle is pointed right at you, Smith, and the shotguns are to make sure your men behave themselves. Now what do you want?"

"I want you for the beating you gave my son," Smith said angrily.

"The only time I laid a hand on your son was when I helped put him in the wagon to take him home."

"How do you explain the broken arm, ribs and bruises?"

"Easy, but you won't believe me."

"That may be the only thing you say that will be the truth."

"Well, I guess you're not interested in the truth. I hope your ranch hands are ready to die. I see no reason not to shoot all of you right now for trespassing. Starting with you, Mr. Smith."

"Wait! Wait!" Mr. Smith said.

"You ready to listen?"

Smith looked around as he thought about what he should do.

"I'll listen," he said softly.

"I had a run-in with your son in town when he tried to physically take Marcie off my wagon. It wasn't enough for him that Marcie told him that she wanted nothing to do with him and never wanted to see him. He didn't like me telling him to leave her alone.

"Your son decided I was responsible for Marcie's feelings. He came here with a gun in his hand, and threatened me with it. By the way, I was unarmed. My horse saw fit to kick him when he walked close behind him. That's how he got so beat up. I took him home."

"I don't believe you,"

"Go home and take a close look at your son's injuries. You will see that his injuries were from a horse kicking him," Fred explained.

"If what you say is true, then I want that horse. A horse like that needs to be destroyed."

"You try to kill that horse, and you will be the next animal to die. It never would have happened if your son had not come here to shoot me."

The men with Mr. Smith lowered their rifles. Even a couple of them put their rifles in their saddle scabbards.

"I think it's time to go home," Smith's foreman said. "I don't want any part of this fight."

"I agree. It's time to go home," one of the men said. "I'll stand for the brand, but not when it's not justified."

"Your son has pestered Miss Marcie for a long time, as long as I've known him. This is all because he isn't getting what he wants," another ranch hand said. "When I get back to the ranch, I'm going to pack my things and leave."

"I'm with you," another ranch hand said.

Mr. Smith turned and looked at his men. It was easy to see that he was thinking. For the first time, he was really beginning to think about his son and his actions. He turned and looked back at Fred. He took a deep breath.

"We'll leave. You will not have any trouble with me, or my son, in the future. I hope this will not affect our doing business in town," Smith said to Bill.

"It will not if your son behaves around my family, and leaves Marcie alone. That means he is not to talk to her at all," Bill said.

Mr. Smith nodded, then turned around and rode away. His men turned and followed him.

The next day, Bill and Fred went out looking for land for Fred to settle on. He found the place he wanted to build his ranch. There was a house on the property, but it needed some work. Marcie helped him fix up the house. As soon as it was ready to live in, Fred asked Marcie to marry him. She said "yes".

Once they were married, they purchased some breeding stock.

Marcie and Fred also raised a family of two girls and two boys. They lived a long time on their ranch in peace.

LONE TREE STATION

Lone Tree Station was nothing more than a small stage stop on a road that crossed the open prairie. From the station, a person could see for miles in all directions, but there was nothing to see but prairie grasslands, an antelope now and then, some buffalo and an occasional dust devil racing across the prairie.

The tree, if you could call it that, was a single small tree about three and half feet tall with only four or five spindly little branches, and not very many leaves. The tree was kept alive by a young widow lady by the name of Mary Sutton, who had managed the station for over a year. She kept the tree alive by watering it during the long hot summer days.

The water for the station came from a small spring out behind the cabin. The spring flowed all year around, no matter what the weather. It was the only source of water at the station, but it was good clean water, and reliable.

The station was a small sod-roofed cabin with only one room. The room consisted of a few chairs around a table, a few cabinets where food and other items such as cups, plates, and cooking pans of various sizes were kept. Off in one corner of the room was a bed with a sheet and a quilt folded over the end of the bed where the widow lady slept, and a small dresser for her personal things.

On the wall near the head of the bed was a gun rack that held a rifle and a shelf where she kept a Colt .45 pistol and a box of ammunition for each. She also kept a shotgun next to the door. All the guns were loaded and ready to use if necessary.

The fireplace at one end of the cabin was used for all the cooking. It was also used to heat the cabin during times of cold weather. Wood used in the fireplace had to be freighted in because there was none anywhere near the station. Every so often, a wagon would bring a load of cut wood. The driver would stack it at the back of station. The wood was provided by the stagecoach company.

Off to the side of the cabin was a corral with a three-sided lean-two to protect the horses owned by the stagecoach company from the sun, wind and rain. There was a small shed just off the side of the corral that was used to keep feed for the horses.

Most of her everyday supplies, like feed for the horses and those things needed to provide meals for the travelers on the stagecoach, were brought to her by the company. Lone Tree Station was a regular stop for a change of horses and to let the passengers get out to stretch their legs and get something to eat.

Other than the stagecoaches stopping on their run across the prairie, Mary Sutton rarely saw anyone. Very little ever happened at Lone Tree Station. The only thing Mary had to keep her busy between stagecoaches stopping, was her small garden out behind the station, where she raised a few vegetables, and her knitting. She was able to raise enough in the garden to can, most of it to help her make it through the winter.

The stagecoaches stopped on every Wednesday about mid-day. They would be going one direction on one Wednesday and the other direction on the next Wednesday. The stagecoaches rarely had more than two passengers, most often only one and occasionally no passengers, just mail and maybe a little freight.

Mary kept very close watch of the days. She had to feed the driver and the man riding shotgun, as well as any passengers when the stagecoaches came by. The meal had to be ready when the stagecoach arrived. The driver and the man riding shotgun changed the horses for her.

One afternoon in mid-July, Mary was hoeing her garden. She stopped to stretch her back and looked out over the prairie. Off in the distance she could see a cloud of dust. She watched it for a minute. At first, she thought it was a dust devil racing across the prairie. It looked like it was coming closer. It wasn't long before she realized it was not a dust devil.

"Today is Monday. There's no scheduled stagecoach today," she said to herself out loud.

She leaned against her garden hoe and put her hand up to shade her eyes as she continued to watch the dust cloud come closer. This is no day to be running a stagecoach that hard, she thought. Besides, it was not Wednesday.

It wasn't until they were closer that she could see it was not a stagecoach. She could see it was four men riding hard toward the station. She dropped her garden hoe and ran to the cabin. As soon as she was inside, she shut the door and locked it. After closing the door, she grabbed the shotgun she kept close to the door. She poked the end of the barrel out the shooting hole in the door and waited.

When the four men rode into the yard in front of the station, she could see that one of the men was hanging onto his saddle while one of the other men led the horse by its reins. It was clear that the man hanging onto his saddle was injured. They didn't look like cowboys, or lawmen.

"You in there, open up."

"You can water your horses and rest them a bit, but then move on."

"I said open the door. We have an injured man here."

"I'll not let you in. I have no idea who you are and why you are here."

"We are not here to harm anyone, ma'am. I'm Marshal Stillwell from over at Red Springs," he said as he pulled his vest back so she could see the badge pinned to his shirt.

"I never heard of you. The injured man looks like he was shot. The way you are riding, I think you are running from someone, probably the law."

"Lady, I am the law. We have no reason to hurt you. We just want to leave him here so, maybe, you can help him.

"We were after some men who killed a rancher. When we caught up with them, we were ambushed in a draw. This was the closest place I could think of where we could get help for my deputy."

"What happened to the men you were after?" she asked.

"They were killed in the gunfight."

"Lady, please, open the door and let us bring my deputy inside" the man pleaded.

The barrel of the shotgun disappeared from the door. The door opened and Mary stepped outside. She was a little nervous, because she wasn't sure these men were who they said they were, but the man who had been shot needed help, and she was the only one within miles of the station who might be able to help him.

"Bring him inside. I will do what I can for him."

Mary stepped aside and watched two of the men carry the injured man inside. She pointed toward the bed. The men laid the deputy on the bed then stepped back out of the way.

Mary went to the man and looked at him. As she opened his shirt to check his wound, she heard the marshal give the men orders to stand watch outside.

She turned and looked at the marshal. She was curious as to why he wanted his men to stand watch. Had they put her in danger by coming there?

"He's hurt pretty bad. I'll do what I can for him, but I don't know if he will live. That hard ride here didn't do him any good.

"I'll need some water. There is a bucket over in the corner. You can get the water from the spring behind the station."

The marshal took the bucket and went outside while Mary took the shirt off the injured man. He returned in a few minutes with the water.

Mary put some water in a pan over the fire to heat it. While it was heating, she cleaned around the wound as much as she could in order to get a better look at the wound. Once the water was hot, she cleaned out the wound. She was glad that the bullet had gone completely through the man's left side. She dressed his wound, then wrapped a long piece of cloth tightly around him to hold the dressing in place and to help stop the bleeding.

"Will he be able to ride by morning?" Stillwell asked.

"Are you kidding. He won't be able to ride a horse for at least a week, maybe longer. If you put him on a horse, he will be lucky to live for more than a mile at the pace you were setting when you came here."

"In that case, we'll have to leave him here."

"I'll take care of him," Mary said. "As soon as he is ready to leave, I'll get a message to you to come and get him."

"I guess that will have to do. We'll be on our way, then."

Mary nodded that she understood, but there was something about the men that puzzled her. Were they who they said they were? She had some doubts. They seemed to be in an awful hurry to get out of there, but she didn't mind. She wanted them gone, and the sooner the better.

When she heard the man who claimed to be a marshal give the order to the other two men to saddle up, he didn't seem to sound much like a marshal, to her way of thinking. She let out a sigh of relief when she heard the horses leave.

She took a quick look outside. The men were riding off in a hurry. The direction they were going was the wrong way to go back to Red Springs.

Mary went back inside and turned her attention to the wounded man they had left behind. She checked the dressing she had put over the man's wound, then covered him with the sheet. He didn't need the quilt; it was already a fairly hot day.

Once she had done all she could for him, she picked up the man's shirt and looked at it. She examined the bullet hole with an eye toward repairing the shirt. There was a bullet hole in it, but from the look of it, he had been shot at close range. It had black powder burns around the hole.

She also noticed something else that gave her pause. There was a tear just above the left shirt pocket. The only thing she could think of that would cause such a tear was something had been pinned to the shirt, then ripped off.

Mary turned and looked toward the door. She wasn't looking at anything as much as she was thinking about the men, especially the one who said he was a marshal. She was also thinking about the two men who brought the injured man into the cabin. The man who was the leader showed her the badge of a marshal. The thought crossed her mind that the wounded man on her bed might actually be the marshal. The other man who had claimed to be the marshal might have torn the badge off the wounded man's shirt so he could pass himself off as the marshal.

Mary wondered if her thought about the man on her bed being the marshal was just her imagination. She looked at him and thought that she would not know if what she was thinking was true or not until he could come around to tell her his name.

The question that crossed her mind was, why would they bring the real marshal to her to take care of? Why would they do that? She had no answers to her questions. She would just have to wait and hope the wounded man lying on her bed would survive his wounds so she could talk to him.

Two days later, the wounded man had still not come around. It was time to get ready for the stagecoach to arrive. She had to get something made for the passengers to eat. She spent most of the morning preparing a meal for the people on the stagecoach, while keeping an eye on the man on her bed.

The stagecoach arrived just shortly before noon. There were two passengers today. They were invited into the station for a meal, but Mary asked them to try not to disturb the injured man on the bed. Though the passengers were curious, they respected her wishes and were quiet while they ate.

After the driver and his partner had changed out the horses, they went inside the station to eat. The driver looked over at the man lying on the bed.

"What's wrong with him?" Stan asked.

"He was brought here the other day by three other men. He had been shot. I have been taking care of him, but he still hasn't come around, yet. Do you happen to know who he is? They never told me his name, and I've never seen him before."

Stan walked over to the bed and looked down at the man. He turned and looked at Mary.

"Why that fella is Marshal John Hooker."

"I had a feeling that the men who brought him here were not lawmen. One of them was wearing his badge."

"Which way did they come from?"

"They rode in from the west and headed east when they left. They brought him in with them, and left him here for me to take care of."

"Was the leader a fairly tall man with a small scar on his right cheek? Did he have sandy colored hair and blue eyes."

"Yes. Yes, he was one of them. From the way he talked to the others, he was the leader."

"That was Stillwell, D. J. Stillwell."

"That was the name he told me, Stillwell. He said he was Marshal Stillwell."

"He's no more a marshal than I am," Stan said. "He is wanted for bank robbery, and killing a bank teller over in Red Springs. He may be wanted for other robberies, but I'm not sure about that."

"He said he was the Marshal in Red Springs. If he robbed the bank in Red Springs, why would he say he was from there? And why would he bring the marshal here?"

"I don't know. He was probably thinking that if you could save the marshal's life, it would help keep him from being hung for killing the marshal. If he is captured, he would probably claim he didn't shoot the marshal. He'll claim one of the others shot him, and he tried to save his life by leaving him here for you to take care of him."

"Do you think that would get him a lighter sentence?" Mary asked.

"He must think so, but they also killed a bystander when they rode out of town."

"I hope they catch them. Sit down, I'm sure you are hungry."

Then Stan and his partner sat down and ate a quick meal. As soon as they finished eating, Stan and his partner got the passengers back into the stagecoach. Stan and his partner got back on the stagecoach, then Stan called out to his horses. The horses lunged forward and the stagecoach left the station.

Mary stood just outside the door as the stagecoach pulled away and continued on its way east. It wasn't long before all she could see was the dust kicked up by the horses and the stagecoach wheels.

She turned and went back inside to clean up the dishes from the noon meal. As she stepped inside, she saw Marshal Hooker looking at her.

"Well, it's about time you woke up. How are you feeling?"

"I feel like I've been shot."

"You have been shot. I suggest that you don't move around much for awhile. I don't want you opening your wound."

"I haven't tried to move."

"Are you hungry?"

"I could eat a little something. Can you tell me where I am?"

"Sure. You are at Lone Tree Station."

"How did I get here? The last thing I remember was someone put me on a horse after I was shot. I remember the jarring I took for a little while, but I don't remember anything after that until I woke just a few minutes ago."

"You were brought here by D.J. Stillwell."

"You're kidding? D.J. Stillwell brought me here?"

"Yes. I'll tell you all about it as soon as I get some broth for you."

Mary got busy cleaning up after the passengers left. She did dishes while she warmed up some broth she had made earlier. As soon as the broth was ready, she took a bowl of it over to a small table next to the bed.

She leaned over John to help him sit up a little and put a pillow behind his head. Mary blushed a little when she saw him looking up at her while she was leaning over him. She was very close to him. Mary quickly sat down on the edge of the bed and began feeding him the broth.

When John had all the broth he wanted, she set the bowl on the bedside table. She gently removed the extra pillow from behind his head, then tucked the sheet around him.

Mary took the bowl and went over to the sink to wash up the bowl and spoon. She turned and was about to ask him if he needed anything only to find that he had gone back to sleep. She smiled then went about her chores.

The next couple of days were very quiet around Lone Tree Station. The routine of the days had returned to the peaceful days Mary often had, except for the fact that she was no longer alone for days on end. She had John to look after.

John was able to get up with Mary's help and sit in a chair. He was not ready to start walking around on his own or to be riding a horse, yet, but he was doing better.

It was a Monday morning and it was already getting hot. As soon as Mary had finished taking care of John, she helped him into a chair next to the door where there was a slight breeze. It wasn't long before John had dozed off.

Since John was asleep, she thought she could go outside for a little while and work in her garden. She had just started to hoe out the weeds when she heard several horses coming toward the station. They were coming from the south.

Mary looked up and saw four Indians coming toward the station. She was concerned until she saw two of them were a couple Indians she knew. It was Little Dove and her brother, Runs Fast, and two other Indians she didn't know. Mary laid down the garden hoe and walked toward the front of the station to greet them.

As the four Indians rode up in front of the station. Mary smiled at them. She had not seen Little Dove for a long time. She raised her hand and smiled.

"Little Dove, it is good to see you. What brings you here?"

"My brother has some news that he wants you to know," she said with a worried tone in her voice.

"Oh. What is the matter?"

"My brother doesn't want me to tell anyone, but I told him we should tell you. You would know what to do."

"Yes, you can tell me anything."

Little Dove looked at her brother, then turned and looked at Mary.

"My brother and his friends found three white men out on the prairie about a two days ride from here. They had been killed by some Indians from another tribe. A tribe that lives mostly in the south, below the big river."

"They were not killed by your people?"

"NO!" she said then took a minute to gather herself.

"There was a fight where they were killed. There were, what you call, bullets, all around them. I do not know what the fight was about, but the three white men had been scalped and their horses taken. Their clothes were taken off them and they were left to bake in the sun."

"Why are you telling me this?"

"We do not want the white man to think anyone from our tribe had done it."

"Can you describe the white men?" John said.

Everyone looked toward the door of the station. Leaning against the door frame was John. He had overheard what was said.

"John, you shouldn't be up."

Little Dove and her brother started to back away. Mary was afraid they would run off.

"Little Dove, don't go. He is a good man. He is a good man."

Little Dove looked first at Mary, then at John. She didn't know what to do."

"Little Dove, please answer him. Can you describe the men?"

Little Dove looked at the others, then back at Mary.

"Please answer him. He will do you no harm."

"One of the men had light colored hair. He was tall."

"Did he have a Marshal's badge on his shirt?" John asked.

Little Dove had a surprised look on her face. She then looked at her brother.

"Yes," she said reluctantly. "We found a shirt with a badge on it near one of the men. My brother took the badge so when the men were found, they would not think we killed what you call a lawman."

"Do you still have the badge?" John asked.

Little Dove looked at her brother and reached out to him. He hesitated for a moment, then gave her the badge. She handed it to Mary. Mary looked at it, then walked over to the door and gave it to John. John looked at the badge, then looked up at Little Dove and smiled.

"Little Dove, thank you for returning my badge to me. The men that were killed were the same men who robbed a bank, killed a bank teller, and wounded me. I can assure you that there will be no one coming after you, or your people."

Little Dove was not sure he meant what he was saying. She looked at Mary.

"It is all right. He is telling you the truth," Mary said.

"You can go in peace," John said with a smile. "And again, thank you."

Little Dove looked at Mary. When Mary smiled and nodded, Little Dove smiled.

Mary and John stood in the door of the station and watched as the Indians rode away. As soon as they were gone, Mary turned and put her arm around John.

"You need to sit down."

"I better before I fall down."

Mary helped him back into the station and helped him sit down on a chair. As she turned away from him, he reached out and took hold of her hand. She turned and looked down at him. She wasn't sure what the look on his face meant.

"Are you all right. You didn't open your wound, did you?"

"No. I don't think so, and I'm fine."

"I think you should rest."

"I agree."

John let go of her, then closed his eyes. He dozed off in the chair.

Mary went out to her garden and picked up her garden hoe. Instead of hoeing her garden, she just stood there thinking about the man who had been in her bed for the past week or so. For the first time in a long time, she had someone other than herself to look after. Having someone to talk to during the long stretches of not seeing anyone, made her feel alive again.

Mary chastised herself for what she was thinking. She liked having him there. She had been alone for a long time. The only time she saw anyone was when the stagecoach stopped, and that was only for twenty to thirty minutes, and occasionally when Little Dove and her brother would stop in, which was not very often.

Time passed slowly while John's wound healed. Gradually, he was able to do a few things around the station to help Mary.

John liked the time he spent with Mary. Although he knew he would have to return to Red Springs, he couldn't help thinking about Mary. He began to think that he might like to stay here and maybe ranch some of the land around the station. The fact he had been shot, tended to make him think about quitting his job as marshal and staying here with Mary. The only real problem was would Mary want him to stay.

The day came when he thought he should return to Red Springs. He went out to the corral and began putting his saddle on his horse.

"Are you leaving?"

"I think I should. I have been away from my job for a long time."

"Will I ever see you again?"

John looked at her. He wasn't sure but he got the feeling that she didn't want him to leave at all.

"Mary, what would you say if I told you that I would like to stay and start a ranch out here - - - with you?"

It was something she had thought about, but didn't know what he would think if she asked him to stay. It was time to give him an answer before he left.

"I would like that. I would like that very much."

"I'm going to go back to Red Springs and turn in my badge. As soon as I have done that, I'll take care of some business I have in Red Springs. I'll buy a wagon and some horses, as well as a few things we would need to start a ranch. What do you think about that?"

"I would like that very much," was all she could think of to say.

John took her in his arms and kissed her gently on the lips. He then stepped back and looked at her. She was looking at him.

"John Hooker, I want you to come back to me."

"I will, I promise."

John took her in his arms, then kissed her again. When he let go of her, she smiled at him.

"I'll be back as soon as I can," he said.

John put his foot in the stirrup and swung into the saddle. He looked down at her for a moment, then turned his horse and rode toward Red Springs.

John went to Red Springs where he reported the death of D.J. Stillwell. He then turned in his badge to the mayor.

After turning in his badge, John went to the Government Land Office and filed claim for a large number of acres around the stage station known as Lone Tree Station. He then bought a wagon, a few horses, and a few things they would need to start a ranch. As soon as he was ready, he returned to Lone Tree Station.

John and Mary got married by a preacher who was passing through the area. Over the years, the ranch grew in size as did the Hooker family. They named the ranch Lone Tree Ranch. The little tree grew to be a big strong cottonwood, and stood proudly in front of the ranch house they built to replace the cabin.

WELLS FARGO ROBBERY

Matt Griswald rode his horse into the town of Deadwood in the Black Hills in the Dakota Territory. He had been on the trail for almost five weeks and was tired. He was looking forward to a warm bath and a shave. After the shave and a good meal, he planned to make a quick stop at a saloon for a drink. Once he had his drink, he was looking forward to a warm bed in one of the nicer hotels for some much-needed rest. Unfortunately, it was beginning to look like his plans may not work out as he hoped they would.

As soon as his foot hit the ground, the local sheriff walked up behind him. Matt turned and looked at the sheriff. He didn't like the sheriff. He had had a few run-ins with him in the past several years, mostly over jurisdictional issues.

"Well, if it isn't Sheriff Delbert Horn. I see you are still sneaking up on people, as usual.

"What are you doing here?" Sheriff Horn asked sharply.

"I'm here to rest for the night, then I'm on my way, hopefully. Not that it is any of your business what I'm doing here."

"You looking for someone here?"

"Nope."

"I find that hard to believe."

"Sorry about that, but that's your problem."

"I hope you're telling me the truth. I don't want any trouble from you." Sheriff Horn said in a threatening tone.

"I don't plan on giving you any trouble, unless you are planning on giving me trouble. Now, if you don't mind, I would like to get my horse over to the livery stable so he can get some rest, and so I can get cleaned up, get a meal and a drink, then get some rest."

Matt didn't wait for the sheriff to respond. He turned his back on the sheriff and led his horse away, leaving the sheriff standing there wondering what Matt's real reason for being in town might be.

As he walked his horse to the livery stable at the blacksmith's shop, he thought about Sheriff Horn. It didn't bother Matt even a little at the way the sheriff treated him. He knew the sheriff didn't like him, but he really didn't have a reason for not liking Matt. It crossed his mind that Sheriff Horn didn't want him in town, but had no idea why.

Once Matt got his horse to the livery stable, he talked to the blacksmith. The blacksmith was to rub Matt's horse down, then put him in a stall and feed him. Matt also requested that he put his horse in a stall where his horse could get some much needed rest. The blacksmith agreed. Matt paid the blacksmith for his services then turned to leave.

"Mr. Griswald?"

Matt stopped, then turned and looked at the blacksmith.

"Yes?"

"Are you going to be staying long?"

"I hadn't planned on it. Why?"

"I feel I should tell you that Sheriff Horn doesn't like you. After you left the last time, he was mad as hell at you."

"Now, why is he so mad at me?"

"He hasn't forgotten that you made him look bad."

"I probably did, but if I hadn't stepped in when I did the last time I was here, he would have been a dead sheriff. A dead sheriff isn't much help to a town like Deadwood. In fact, a dead sheriff isn't much help to anyone."

"Most of the people who live here know you saved his bacon. A lot of people in this town sorta wished you hadn't saved him. He's not liked all that well here."

"Well, I guess he will just have to be mad at me for 'saving his bacon' as you kindly put it. However, if he gives me too much trouble during the short time I plan to be here, you may have to find a new sheriff, anyway," Matt said with a slight grin.

"Yes. sir. I understand," the blacksmith said with a grin.

"Thanks for the warning. I'll do my best to stay out of his way. I'll mind my own business. As long as he doesn't interfere with me, we won't have a problem."

"Yes, sir. How long do you expect to be in town?"

"As of this moment, I'm not sure. I hope to leave tomorrow morning, but that might change."

"I'll have your horse all rested up so he is ready to travel when you are."

"Thank you," Matt said.

Matt left the blacksmith's shop and walked down the street toward the hotel. He saw Sheriff Horn standing across the street leaning against a post in front of one of the saloons. It was obvious to Matt that he was watching him. Matt wasn't sure why the sheriff was so interested in what he was doing. He wondered if it had something to do with the real reason he was here.

Matt reached up and touched the brim of his hat and nodded slightly to make sure the sheriff knew he had been seen. He smiled to himself as he continued down the street. When he got to the Franklin Hotel, he turned and went inside. There was a handsome young woman at the front desk. He walked up and set his rifle on the counter.

"I'd like a bath, a shave and a quiet room for the night, please."

"Yes sir. Your bath will be ready in about fifteen minutes. We will call for you at your room. Please sign the register," the young woman said as if she had said it a hundred times a day.

Matt picked up the pen and signed his name, then turned the register around so she could read his name. She looked at the register, then looked up at Matt.

"Oh, Mr. Griswald. Welcome to the Franklin Hotel. If there is anything we can do for you to make your stay a pleasant one, simply let us know," she said with a smile.

"A key to my room, and a bath will do for now, thank you."

"Yes, sir."

She turned around and took a key off the wall and handed it to him. He thanked her, then turned and went to the stairs.

His room was on the second floor at the front of the hotel. As he entered the room, he could see there was a window that overlooked the street below. He walked over to the side of the window and peeked out. Matt was looking to see if anyone might be watching him. He wasn't disappointed. He saw Sheriff Horn across the street. The sheriff was looking at the hotel.

While Matt was watching Sheriff Horn, a man walked up next to the sheriff. They talked for a minute or two, then the sheriff walked away, leaving the man standing in the doorway of a building across the street. It was clear that the sheriff was having him watched.

Matt pulled back away from the window. He didn't want the man watching him to know he had been spotted. His thoughts were interrupted suddenly by a knock on the door.

"Who is it?"

"Your bath is ready, sir."

Matt grabbed his gun and went to the door. Holding the gun slightly behind him, Matt opened the door. There was a man standing there smiling.

"Your bath is ready. It's in room A, the third door on the right just down the hall. There are towels for you over the back of the chair in the room. Is there anything else we can do for you?"

"No. Thank you."

Matt closed the door, then picked up the clean clothes he planned to wear. With his gun held under his clean clothes, he opened the door and looked out. There was no one in the hall. He walked down the hall to room A. After checking the hallway, he opened the door to room A. Seeing no one in the room, he entered the room and closed the door.

He laid his gun on the small table next to the tub, then got ready to get in the tub. Matt reached out and touched the water in the tub. He found the water to be warm, just the way he liked it. He got in the tub. He scrubbed up. It felt good to have a chance to take a bath after several days of riding across the open prairie and on into the Black Hills.

He wasn't sure how long he had been in the tub when there was a knock on the door. He reached over and picked up his gun.

"Who is it?"

"I'm checking to see if you need some more hot water."

It was a woman's voice he heard. He knew that it was common for women to bring water while the man was bathing, especially in this town.

"Come in."

He watched as the door opened. Matt was ready just in case it was someone other than the woman with hot water. He watched as the young woman came in with a bucket of hot water. She was surprised to see a gun pointed at her. She stopped and stared at the gun. Matt quickly put the gun on the table next to the tub.

"Sorry. I didn't mean to frighten you."

She hesitated a moment before she moved up close to him. She continued to look at him while she added some hot water to the tub. As soon as she had emptied the bucket of hot water, she stepped back.

"Thank you. I'm sorry that I frightened you."

"I was startled a bit, but I shouldn't have been. I know who you are. I also know that you are nice to women."

"It is nice of you to say that. I try to be respectful of women."

"I noticed Sheriff Horn followed you here."

"How did you see that?"

"I was making up your room and saw him across the street. Is he afraid of you?"

"Let me put it this way, he doesn't like me. It seems I embarrassed him awhile back."

"Oh, I think I heard something about that."

"I think the whole town has heard about it." Matt said with a smile.

"Are you a lawman?"

"Not really."

"Can you tell me why you are here if you know that the sheriff doesn't like you and is following you?"

"I'm here to get a bath, a shave and a good meal. I also plan on getting a good night's sleep."

"Then why is the sheriff having someone watching you all the time?"

"I don't know. Maybe he thinks I'm here to cause him trouble, but I'm not. Why is he following me? You will have to ask him that."

"Oh.," she said as she smiled. "I understand. You don't want anyone to know why you are here. Am I right?"

"Right. I don't want anyone to know that I'm even here. The sheriff knows I'm here, you know I'm here, and the blacksmith knows I'm here. So I guess the secret is out. I'm here," he said with a slight chuckle.

"All I want is a warm bath, a shave, a good meal, and a warm bed to sleep in before I leave, hopefully in the morning. That is why I'm here," Matt said with a smile.

"Yes sir. If there is anything I can do for you, just let me know."

"I will, and thank you."

"He watched her leave. As soon as she was gone, he finished washing, then got out of the tube and dried himself off. He got dressed then left the hotel. He walked down the street to the barber shop where he got a shave and his hair trimmed.

On his way back to the hotel, he stopped off at the Silver Dollar Saloon and had a drink. Since he had done what he told the sheriff he was going to do, he returned the hotel and went straight to his room. It was now time to wait and get a little rest before he went to the Wells Fargo Company office.

Matt didn't sleep very long. When he woke, he noticed that it would not be long before it would be getting dark. He got up and peeked out the side of the window. There was a man standing in front of the building across the street from the hotel. He smiled thinking that the man would be standing there a very long time. It was time to put his plan into action.

As he put on his gun, he moved over to the window and peeked outside just to make sure the man was still there. The man was still standing across the street looking at the hotel. Matt smiled as he thought the man across the street looked bored to death just watching a hotel.

Matt turned and went to the door of his room. He slowly opened the door and checked the hall. There was no one in the hall. He slipped out of his room and down the hall to the backstairs. He went down the stairs, then slipped out the back of the hotel.

He moved along behind the buildings until he came to the back of the Wells Fargo Office. Matt lightly knocked on the backdoor. He kept a sharp lookout for anyone who might see him, but he saw no one.

He turned and looked as the door began to open. There was a man in a suit looking out at him.

The man motioned for Matt to come in. As Matt passed the man, the man looked up and down the area behind the building. He stepped back in and shut the door.

"It is good to see you, Matt."

"It's good to see you, James. What's going on that you wanted to see me without anyone knowing about it?"

"We have been having small amounts of gold taken from our office."

"What do you mean by 'small amounts'? What do you consider a small amount"?

"It amounts to about five hundred to six hundred dollars worth of gold after we receive a shipment of gold to be sent to the mint in Denver. It has totaled up to close to one hundred thousand dollars in gold so far."

"How do you know it is being taken from here?"

"First of all, the gold is weighed before it leaves the mine, by the mining company. When it gets here, we weigh it again. If the weights are the same, we except the shipment. By the way, it has always been the same. Since we ship it ourselves, it isn't weighed again until it is weighed at the mint in Denver."

Matt looked at James for a minute, just thinking about what he had been told. He could see only two places where some of the gold could be removed from the shipment.

"So, some of the gold is being removed from the shipment between the time it arrives here, and it arrives at the mint. How is it shipped from here?"

"By stagecoach. By the way, in our own stagecoaches with our own drivers and guards. It is not always the same drivers and guards. I will vouch for the drivers and guards." James said.

"Have you tried weighing the gold just before it is loaded on the stagecoaches?" Matt asked.

"Why would we do that? When the gold arrives, it's weighed, then put in a safe. It stays in the safe until we load it directly onto the stagecoaches.

"Is there anyone, other than yourself, who knows that I'm here to see you?"

"No. That's why I wanted you to come to see me by the backdoor. I knew you would come see me when you got to town. By now, almost everyone knows you are in town, but they don't know why you are here."

"According to your letter, you should have received a shipment of gold this morning. Is that correct?" Matt asked.

"Yes. We did receive the gold on schedule. It was weighed just like we always do. Then it was put in the safe. I over saw all of it myself."

"Do you keep a guard on duty all night?"

"Yes. We have a guard here in the office while the gold is in the safe."

"Is it the same guard every night?"

"No. We have two different guards. It hasn't mattered which guard was on duty. We still end up missing about the same amount from each shipment."

Matt took a few minutes to think about what he had been told. How were they getting the gold out of the office? How many people were involved? Those were two questions that came to Matt's mind.

"Is there some place I can hide in here where the guard will not know I'm here?"

"Do you think the gold is being stolen right here in the office?"

"There are only two places where it can be stolen, from what you have told me. Here, or while it is transported by stagecoach to Denver. If your shipment is light when it reaches the mint, and it is not touched, we will know that someone is taking it between here and the mint.

"I see you point. You can hide in my closet. From there you can see the safe."

"Okay. I'm going to return to the hotel and sneak back in, then go out the front door of the hotel where I will be seen. I will have dinner then return to the hotel. I'll sneak out of the hotel and come here by the backdoor. I'll hide in the closet all night. I'll see what happens tonight."

"Okay."

"The key to this working, is no one must know that I will be in your office."

"I understand. You best get out of here before anyone sees you now," James said.

"I'll see you later."

James went to the backdoor and looked outside. He didn't see anyone, so he motioned for Matt to leave. Matt slipped out and walked back to the hotel.

When he got back to the hotel, he went up the backstairs and down the hall to his room without being seen. Matt moved over to the side of the window and peeked out. He smiled when he saw the man still standing in front of the building across the street.

He decided to relax for a little while. He laid down on the bed, but didn't go to sleep. He simply rested while he thought about what he was going to do tonight. He worked out in his head every step he would take to avoid being seen by anyone.

When it was getting close to dinnertime, Matt got up and left the hotel by the front door. Out of the corner of his eye he could see a different man across the street in a doorway watching him.

Matt went down the street to a café. He turned in and sat down at a table. He ordered a meal, then relaxed while he enjoyed his meal. Matt could see the man who had been following him. He was across the street standing in front of one of the many saloons.

After he finished his meal, Matt got up and walked out of the café. He stopped. He looked up and down the street as if he was trying to decide where he was going to go next.

The man following him was still across the street. He wasn't very good at staying back in the shadows because Matt spotted him right away.

Matt turned, then walked down the street to a saloon. He went inside and sat down at a table. He could see the man who had been following him was still across the street.

A nice looking young woman walked up to Matt's table and smiled at him.

"You looking for company tonight?" she asked.

"Not really, but if you want to sit down, I'll buy you a drink."

The woman smiled, then pulled back a chair and sat down. The bartender came over to the table.

"What'll it be."

"I'll have a beer," Matt said. "and get the young lady whatever she wants to drink."

"I'll have a whisky," she said,

"By the way, what is your name?" Matt asked the woman as the bartender walked away.

"Mary Bell."

Matt sat with Mary Bell for over an hour. Although it looked like he was simply enjoying a drink and conversation with her, Matt was keeping an eye on the man across the street who had been following him.

"Mary Bell, how would you like to earn about twenty dollars?"

"Sure. What do I have to do?"

"I want you to come to my room at the Franklin Hotel with me. I want you to spend the night in my room."

"That sounds like it could be interesting," she said with a smile.

"It certainly could be."

"You don't want me to do anything weird, do you?" she asked.

"No, not at all. I do have one question to ask you that may seem strange."

"What's that?"

"Do you like Sheriff Horn?"

"No. He treats all the girls around here as if they are his personal property. None of the girls like him. Are you planning on playing some sort of trick on him?"

"You might say that."

"I'm in. When do we start?" she said with a hint of excitement in her voice.

"As soon as you finish your drink."

After they finished their drinks, Matt took Mary Bell by the arm and left the saloon. They walked with their arms around each other to the Franklin Hotel, then on up to his room.

Once in the room, Matt lit the lamp on the table next to the bed. He told Mary Bell what he wanted her to do.

He led her close to the window, then drew her close. He kissed her. He then blew out the lamp so the room was dark.

"I'm going to leave now. I want you to stay here until I get back. It may be most of the night. If you like, you can go to sleep. Whatever you do, do not leave this room until the sun comes up. Got it?"

"Yeah. This is the first time someone has taken me to his room, then left," she said with a smile.

"Here is the twenty dollar gold piece. There will be another twenty dollar gold piece if you stay here all night."

"I'll be right here," she said with a smile.

"Good. Sleep well," Matt said then left the room.

Being very careful not to be seen, Matt worked his way over to the Wells Fargo office. He lightly tapped on the backdoor. James opened it.

Matt slipped in then went directly to the closet. James had been nice enough to put a chair in the closet for Matt to sit on.

Matt had only been there for a short time when he heard someone come in. He listened.

"Come in," James said.

"We got another shipment today?" the man asked.

"Yeah. I've locked the backdoor. Make yourself comfortable. I'll lock the front door on my way out. Keep a sharp eye out. I'll see you in the morning." James said.

Matt heard the front door shut and lock. James was gone. It was time to wait and see what happened.

Time passed slowly. The only thing Matt could see was the faint glow of a single lamp that was out on the counter at the front of the office.

Matt wasn't sure how long he had been in the closet when he heard someone lightly knock on the front door. The next thing he heard was the front door being unlocked. He heard the door open then being closed and locked.

"You think this is a good idea with that Griswald fella being in town?"

It was easy for Matt to recognize the voice he heard. It was that of the guard. Matt had heard his voice when he came in.

"Yeah. He is busy with that pretty little gal from the Gold Pan Saloon."

It was the second voice that got Matt's attention. It was the voice of Sheriff Horn.

"You sure he's there?"

"Yeah. Will saw him take her to his room in the hotel. He's watching to see if he leaves the hotel. Let's get at it. I don't want to be here any longer than I need to be."

Matt could hear them walk over to the safe. He opened the closet door just enough to see what they were doing. The guard was opening the safe. As soon as it was opened, the two men began taking small amounts of gold out of each of the boxes containing the gold from the mine."

"Why don't we just take it all and get out of here? We could be gone and out of the territory before it is even missed."

"We could do that, but then we would be on the run for a long time. This way we get the gold and no one knows a thing about it."

Matt listened to the two men. If it wasn't the same guard each time the gold was missing, the other guard had to be in on it, too, Matt thought. It was clear to Matt that if he took them now, he would get the head man. Even if the second guard got off, or got away, they would still have the leader.

Matt could see that they had their backs to him. It was time to take them into custody.

Matt slowly opened the closet door. With his gun in his hand, he stepped out of the closet.

"Hands up," Matt said.

Suddenly the guard swung around while drawing his gun. Matt quickly shot him. He noticed that Sheriff Horn was looking like he was going to draw, but hesitated. With Matt's gun pointed at him, he decided against it.

"Good move on your part," Matt said. "Turn around."

As soon as he turned around, Matt took the sheriff's gun from his holster. He emptied it then put it back in the sheriff's holster.

"We are going to walk down to the hotel and get the man you had following me."

"You won't live to get me in jail," Sheriff Horn said.

"We'll see about that. Keep your hands at your sides, and get moving. One wrong move from you or any of your men and I'll shoot you first," Matt said. "Just in case you're thinking of trying something, this .45 will shatter your spine."

"You won't shoot me in the back," he said.

"I won't have a second thought about shooting you in the back. Now start moving."

Matt opened the front door of the Wells Fargo Office. He marched the sheriff out the door and onto the boardwalk.

They started down the boardwalk toward the jail. The way to the jail would take them right past the man who had been watching Matt's room at the hotel.

When they got close to the man who had been watching Matt's room, Matt stopped. He put the end of the barrel of his pistol against Sheriff Horn's head while Matt stood behind the sheriff.

"Drop your gun, NOW," Matt said.

The man looked at Horn as if he didn't know what to do.

"I said, 'Drop your gun.'"

"You better drop your gun. He means it. He will kill me then you."

Reluctantly, the man dropped his gun.

"Now put your hands on your head and turn around. If you take your hands off your head, I will shoot you.

The man did as he was told. Matt didn't have to tell them what to do next. The man turned around and started toward the jail with Sheriff Horn and Matt following along.

Once inside the jail, Matt locked up Horn and the man who had been watching him. After locking them up, Matt sat down at the sheriff's desk. He sent out a message on the telegraph wire to nearby Fort Meade requesting a military escort for prisoners to Pierre as soon as possible.

It wasn't long before the local mayor showed up at the jail. Matt told him what was going on, and that he had arrested them.

"You can't just come walking in here and arrest our duly elected sheriff," the mayor said. "Under what authority do you have to arrest the sheriff?"

"Under the authority of the Head Territorial Marshal, Jack Monday. Your so-called sheriff has been stealing gold from Wells Fargo for the past two years. He and his friends will be taken to Pierre under military escort for trial. They will be tried in Pierre, under territorial authority, not local authority.

"So, you're a Territorial Marshal?"

"Not really. I am under contract to Jack Monday for the purpose of catching those involved in the theft of government gold from Wells Fargo and Company."

The mayor just looked at Matt for a moment, then turned and walked away. Matt stayed seated behind the sheriff's desk to wait for the Military escort to arrive. He now had the job of watching over his prisoners until they were turned over to the military escort.

Just as Matt was putting his feet up on the desk in the hope of getting a little rest, the door to the Sheriff's Office opened. He looked up and saw Mary Bell come through the door. He quickly stood up.

"I heard you were busy last night," she said with a smile.

"Yes, I was. I guess I owe you a twenty dollar gold piece."

"No, you don't, but a nice breakfast with you would be nice."

"Yes, it would. But I can't leave just yet."

"I'll go to the café and get us breakfast and bring it here," she said.

While she was gone, the military escort showed up. Matt watched as the prisoners were shackled and place in a prison wagon. The prison wagon left for Pierre just as Mary Bell showed up with breakfast.

"Was that the Army?" Mary Bell asked.

"Yes, it was."

"Did I see the sheriff in the back of that prison wagon?" she asked with a surprised look on her face.

"Yes," Matt said with a smile on his face.

"Wait'til I tell the girls that the sheriff was hauled off in a prison wagon."

"Would you mind waiting to tell them until after we have had our breakfast?"

She smiled then set their breakfast on the desk. Mary Bell sat down across the desk from Matt. They enjoyed their breakfast. When they were done, Matt gave her the twenty dollar gold piece he had promised her.

"Thanks," she said. "What are you going to do now?"

"I'm going to the Well Fargo office and visit with James. I need to report to him what happened. Once I'm done with that, I will be returning to Pierre. I will be there until after the trial of Delbert Horn, the ex-sheriff of Deadwood."

"That 'ex-sheriff of Deadwood' sounds good," Mary Bell said. "What are you doing after the trial."

"You never know. I might just come back here."

"I hope you do. Will I see you if you come back?"

"You can count on it."

Mary Bell smiled then turned and left the office. Matt followed her out.

Matt went on down the street to the Wells Fargo office. He told James what happened, then went to the Blacksmith's shop. After talking briefly to the blacksmith, he got his horse and headed for Pierre.

Trial was held in Pierre. During the trial, it was discovered that the two men who had been watching Matt for the sheriff at different times were the same two men who had been guards at the Wells Fargo Office. One of them was killed by Matt at the Wells Fargo Office. Delbert Horn and the man Matt had captured while taking Sheriff Horn to jail were found guilty of robbery. They were sentenced to ten years at hard labor in the state prison.

It was also discovered during the trial that Delbert Horn had killed a young cowboy just because he didn't like the cowboy for trying to get one of the dance hall girls to go to bed with him. Horn considered the girl his personal property.

Horn was also tried for the murder of the cowboy and found guilty. He was sentenced to hang. He was hung at the state prison.

Matt Griswald returned to Deadwood. He spent a few days, and nights, with Mary Bell before he went to his next assignment.

Made in the USA
Middletown, DE
25 March 2022

63159846R00086